YOUNG CAPTAIN NEMO

YOUNG CAPTAIN NEMO

JASON HENDERSON

Feiwel and Friends

NEW YORK

A Feiwel and Friends Book
An imprint of Macmillan Publishing Group, LLC
Young Captain Nemo. Copyright © 2019 by Jason Henderson. All rights reserved.

Printed in the United States of America by LSC Communications,
Harrisonburg, Virginia. For information, address Feiwel and Friends,
175 Fifth Avenue, New York, NY 10010.

Our books may be purchased in bulk for promotional, educational, or business use.
Please contact your local bookseller or the Macmillan Corporate and Premium Sales
Department at (800) 221-7945 ext. 5442 or by email at
MacmillanSpecialMarkets@macmillan.com.

Library of Congress Cataloging-in-Publication Data

Names: Henderson, Jason, 1971- author.
Title: Young Captain Nemo / Jason Henderson.
Description: First edition. | New York : Feiwel and Friends, 2019. |
    Series: Young Captain Nemo ; [1] | Summary: Seventh-grader Gabriel Nemo,
    the famous Captain Nemo's descendant, and his friends Peter and Misty save
    sinking ships, face mutant sea creatures, and more while eluding the Navy
    and Peter and Misty's parents.
Identifiers: LCCN 2018019096 (print) | LCCN 2018027766 (ebook) |
    ISBN 9781250173225 (hardcover) | ISBN 9781250173232 (eBook)
Subjects: CYAC: Adventure and adventurers—Fiction. | Submarines
    (Ships)—Fiction. | Rescue work—Fiction. | Mutation (Biology)—Fiction. |
    Underwater exploration—Fiction. | Science fiction.
Classification: LCC PZ7.H37955 (ebook) | LCC PZ7.H37955 You 2019 (print) |
    DDC [Fic]—dc23
LC record available at https://lccn.loc.gov/2018019096

BOOK DESIGN BY KATIE KLIMOWICZ

Feiwel and Friends logo designed by Filomena Tuosto

First edition, 2019
1 3 5 7 9 10 8 6 4 2
mackids.com

For Minerva Trujillo of Killeen, Texas, the best teacher I ever had

YOUNG CAPTAIN NEMO

LIKE YOU, I AM WILLING TO LIVE OBSCURE.

—*Captain Nemo*

PROLOGUE

Four hundred miles off the coast of California, the enormous submarine *Nebula* needed to make repairs. Its captain had made a horrible mistake. Nerissa Nemo paced back and forth in front of the view screen on the bridge of the ship and tried to hide from her crew that she was angry, mostly at herself. She watched the ocean waves outside going from black to gray to soft, translucent blue-green, until suddenly they saw the sun and the two-hundred-foot ship broke the surface to rest.

"Full stop," Nerissa said to the helmsman. She felt dozens of stabilizers along the belly of the ship kick in, steadying it as they held its place. "What's the damage?"

Jaideep, her executive officer, looked over a crewman's shoulder at one of the consoles and read with a pair of reading glasses he pulled from his shirt pocket. "Engines are one hundred percent; that's the good news. The bad news is we have hull breaches in four different places, plus the machinery in the battering nose is offline."

They had no choice but to stop. Nerissa Nemo could spin the last six hours any way she wanted, but it all came out to catastrophe.

She had followed a lead on a ship carrying whale oil and other substances harvested through the illegal killing of whales protected by international law. Nerissa knew that some people were still allowed to hunt—Alaskan Inuit and the like—and she had no problem with small populations carrying on their traditions. But modern, technological whaling was a crime. Not that Nerissa normally cared much about the law. But in this case the law was right. The criminals were slaughtering gray whales on the whim of some very rich people for things they could easily make on land now. The buyers in Baja California, Mexico, were expected to pay millions. So she had attacked the smugglers' boat. Tried to ram it. That was what she did. That was what made the oceans safer one ship at a time, and what put a fantastic price on her eighteen-year-old head.

But this boat had been a trap. A fake. They had just gotten near it when the smugglers' ship exploded like a floating bomb—just waiting for her. She had escaped at the last minute. Barely.

And now they were going to spend an hour fixing the

holes in the *Nebula*'s hull, and all told she was lucky that it wasn't worse.

Someone had tried to kill her. And that someone was going to regret failing.

She angrily bit her lip. "I'll be in my quarters." Nerissa stomped away from the view screen as the crew set about planning the repairs.

She'd made it a few steps when the whole ship rocked hard to port. Nerissa was thrown off balance and fell to the left as the deck tilted sharply. She caught hold of a workstation as the *Nebula* shuddered and righted itself.

"We collided with something!" Nerissa shouted to Jaideep. "What was that?"

Her second-in-command didn't answer at first, silent and transfixed by a great shadow moving across the view screen. "I can't tell."

The image view flickered and couldn't seem to stay focused. Apparently the camera had been damaged in the explosion. A long, dark shadow moved across the corner of the hazy image. Nerissa couldn't tell precisely what it was, but the whack it had given them told her it was a ship. Normally they could have handled a collision, but with the ruptures from the explosion they were weakened already. So was this a second part of the same attack?

That didn't seem likely. But something was moving around them.

"Calm waters," the helmsman reported. The view

screen filled with four different camera angles showing the whole of the ship. Water ran off the long walkway along the top of the sub, and the steel railings glistened wet in the floodlights. Beyond the sub flashing in its own light, an endless black blanket of sky stretched and shimmered with countless stars.

"Do we see the ship that hit us?"

The helmsman brought a sonar image up in the corner of the view screen. The green wand swept around, showing only themselves.

"Wait a few minutes. Then let's get the crews moving…" She stopped as something appeared on the sonar screen as a large dot moving away from them. "It came up from below. Get the cameras on it," Nerissa ordered.

The starboard camera swiveled and magnified.

A bulbous rise in the water was moving steadily away from them, its wake still showing its path from underneath the ship. The shape under the water was long and round, causing the lift in the water. "It looks like a torpedo."

"It's too big for a torpedo," Jaideep observed.

"You're right, you're right." Nerissa watched the thing go. "It's huge, like a ballistic missile."

"Nothing can fire that big a missile from underwater at that angle," Jaideep said.

"And anyway, missiles don't run away." She leaned on the station in front of her. *What are you?* Nerissa spun around.

"I'm going up for a better look." She gestured for Jaideep to follow and turned to the helmsman. "Helm, you have the bridge."

By *up* she meant *topside*, climbing a ladder and heading out on top of the submarine as it floated on the surface. They ran out of the bridge to the end of a long corridor, and Nerissa unclipped a pair of binoculars from a supply rack next to the ladder before beginning to climb. The hatch to topside unlocked with her palm print and seemed to take forever, but finally it opened up like an iris and she was out.

Out in the wind and the waves. Nerissa had always loved being topside, up on the railing, the great ship rocking, just Nerissa, her ship, and the stars. Salt air misted Nerissa's face as she stepped forward, her boots skidding slightly on the perilously slick platform—they couldn't have rough textures on the surface for fear of causing vibrations that listening ships might hear. Even the waist-high railings she gripped tightly to steady herself were tapered at the ends to cut through the water in silence.

Balancing against the rail, Nerissa peered across the water in the direction the object had gone. But there was nothing.

Water splashed loudly behind her.

"Captain, *there*." Jaideep pointed and she twisted around. Now it was on the other side of the ship. It had dived under them again and was moving away once more, in the other direction.

Ships didn't do that, swim back and forth under you. *Whales* did, but this was obviously mechanical.

"It's fast," Jaideep observed. "Submarine, maybe?"

But she could see it better now. "That's no submarine." Through the water, she could make out the flat-painted metal of the main body with two odd shapes on either side... almost like pontoons. "But someone is definitely having fun with us." It bothered her that this thing had appeared right after someone had tried to blow her up. But nothing about this craft—if it *was* a craft—seemed to be the work of an angry government or smuggling operation.

Could it be some kind of spy vessel? If so, why would it be playing around with the *Nebula* like this?

Then it moved in a way that her brain couldn't understand, and her blood ran cold. It seemed to *flex*, the side pontoons, or whatever they were, moving up and down in the water as if it were swimming.

"It's not a ship and it's not a machine," she said. "It's an *animal*. We need to get tags—" She was cut off by an unearthly sound, a high-pitched, watery call that filled the air. A call, like a whale's after all, or some other large creature's. But what was with all the metal?

She gasped in awe as a rushing whirlpool formed around the nose of the creature. It tilted up, whipping around to point toward them. The high call continued as the strange animal-and-metal thing rose out of the water and *took flight*.

It soared into the air, water erupting all around it as the creature flapped its wings.

Wings!

Nerissa gaped, trying to process what she was seeing. For that's what they *were*: long metal wings attached to a gray fuselage, with big dead engines in the middle of each wing. It was an *airplane* with a great glass cockpit, half the glass broken and streaming water and gunk. And bulging from every seam were tentacles, countless ropy, fleshy protuberances that moved constantly.

She couldn't see the nose properly as it rose, but the writing on the tail was visible now: *Fighting Irish*, in English, and the red, white, and blue of the American flag.

"Those—those are World War Two markings," Nerissa realized. "It's American! It's a B-17."

"A *what?*" Jaideep shouted. The creature turned in the air as it rose, shining wet against the starry sky. It spun like a whale, water spraying off the countless tendrils waving out of open seams up and down its body.

All throughout, it continued a long, high-pitched, gurgling whine unlike anything she'd ever heard.

"A *B-17 airplane*," Nerissa repeated. It had to be, what, eighty years old? But *how?* She looked up and bounced on her heels, feeling giddiness in her chest as she called loudly, "What *are* you? Let us *see* you!"

"Um, Captain," Jaideep said, "is calling that thing a good idea?"

And now as if in answer it nodded its head and started coming down, flipping over in the air, gravity taking it as it soared toward the walkway of the *Nebula.*

There was no time to get inside. It was coming down fast.

Nerissa looked into the *face* of the silver beast. The glass cockpit was split open, and out of it thrust a mollusk-like forehead—at least that was how she thought of it—and below that an open mouth with hundreds of long, thin, whalelike teeth.

It's playing, she thought, but she had no idea if it had any sense not to crush them. She held up her arms involuntarily, seeing herself squashed across the platform with Jaideep.

But the creature whipped its wings as it came down. Relief flooded through her body as it leveled off and flew over the platform so close that she could smell the gunk of the thing. The B-17 slipped through the air, roaring its strange whining roar, and plunged into the water on the other side of the ship.

"Fantastic!" Nerissa shouted as she ran down the walkway, trying to see where it had gone.

Off the starboard side, the creature swam away from them in its original direction, still close under the water.

"Come back," she whispered. "I need another look." Nerissa bounced on her heels again. Mentally she was half in her own body, half in some unplaceable library of her mind, flipping through everything she knew about the sea. There was nothing out there like this that she had seen or heard of. *Nothing.*

"Come *on!*"

But the mound of water, so much like a torpedo speeding away, slowed and then dove, its metal tail kicking up as it plunged into the icy sea and was gone.

"Captain, what *was* that thing?" Jaideep sounded a lot less excited than Nerissa.

Nerissa swore and slapped the railing. "I have *literally* no idea. It's *amazing.*"

She raised her binoculars and swept clean around again, looking for any sign of its return. After several minutes she lowered the glasses. Her blood was pumping. *Come back*, she wanted to shout. *Let us know you.*

Finally Jaideep spoke again. "Captain? Orders?"

Nerissa nodded. "Start the repairs. And find me an intelligence officer. We're gonna crack into every system on earth. If anyone else has seen that thing, I want to know about it."

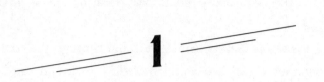

GABRIEL NEMO GLANCED around as he chained his bicycle to a secluded bike rack behind the Santa Marta Aquarium. No one had noticed him arrive alone. He secured the lock—a design he had worked on himself—with his thumbprint and heard a satisfying chirp as the tumblers slid into place.

The salt-sea air off the Pacific lifted the collar of his dark-green jacket as he made his way toward the front. He checked his watch. Six P.M. Right on time. He rounded the edge of the enormous glass-and-steel structure, rehearsing everything he would say about why his parents weren't there, as the clanking sounds of the marina and the roar of the ocean gave way to the chattering of his classmates.

In his ear, a tiny radio receiver droned on with news of the sea, and he listened for a moment.

"*Sqrrk.* Sitrep on the container vessel?"

"*Sqrrk.* Still have containers floating for a quarter mile..."

As far as Gabriel could work out through the static, a container vessel had collided with a dock and capsized. The crew had already been evacuated, but the seashore and shallows there were a mess and the coast guard had been calling in help for hours.

A mess, but all in all a routine cleanup from the sounds of it. Nothing that needed Gabriel or his skills. He had decided to come here tonight instead. To fit in. To be normal.

Even so, he didn't take the Nemotech receiver out of his ear. Just in case. With any luck, he might be needed... which was a thought he didn't like to examine too closely, because it meant he considered the idea of something terrible happening to be *lucky*.

Gabriel fell in with the parade of middle school students and parents making its way through the entrance. Gabriel scanned the faces until he saw his friend Peter Kosydar and his mom. They had stopped just to the right of the double doors under a long white banner that read HARRISON STEM SEVENTH GRADE AUCTION TONIGHT!

"Gabe!" Peter waved and his mom did, too. Gabriel cut

through the crowd to join his friend, mentally pushing away the radio sounds in his ear.

Peter's mom was a hugger, so she wrapped Gabriel in a bone-crusher that left him feeling squashed, then stepped back, her arms on his shoulders. She beamed at Gabriel from under a big, floppy hat. Ms. Kosydar had freckles that reminded Gabriel of his sister, and he felt a sudden pang of sadness. He hadn't seen anyone in his family in months, much less *her.*

"Are your parents here?" Ms. Kosydar asked. "I've been wanting to meet them."

That was what he'd been afraid of, and it was the first thing his friend's mom had asked: *Where are your parents?* The answer was *A long way from here.* He didn't like to think about it and didn't like to lie about it. The whole thing, as much as he hated to admit it to himself, made him sad. After all, *It's okay, they sent me here by myself* would only raise more questions. When he had first arrived, he'd had the *best* time by himself. He could do anything he wanted, go to bed at any time at all, eat anything. He was king of his own life. The good time had lasted about forty-eight hours.

Still, he had his extracurricular activities. Maybe that made it worth it. Maybe.

"They might make it later." Gabriel smiled and tried not to let his sadness leak all the way to his eyes. Instead he changed the subject. "Peter, did you hear they have a new jellyfish habitat? They use rotors to simulate ocean currents. You know, so they stay up and you can see them."

"*Oh* yeah." Peter pushed up his glasses, and the boys stepped into the enormous foyer of the aquarium. Above them, the skeleton of a whale hung suspended from a far-off ceiling through which they could see the stars. "Did you know a guy got stung last week? How stupid can you get?"

"I'm sure they're not stupid," Ms. Kosydar said.

"Oh, they have rules to follow. But if you don't wear the right gloves... *bzzt.*" Peter imitated a guy receiving an electrical jolt, and Gabriel cracked up.

"Of course—" Ms. Kosydar interjected.

"Of course that's not what jellyfish do." Peter rolled his eyes as he cut his mom off. "But it's hard to do an impression of a jellyfish sting without, you know, falling down and screaming." Peter knew his marine biology—he wasn't crazy for it like Gabriel was (Peter's fascination ran to navigation, vehicles, *movement*), but they couldn't spend as much time together as they did without Peter being able to run rings around your average student.

"Hello!" Mrs. Holsted, the assistant principal at Harrison, spoke into a microphone from where she stood on a stage at the back of the room. She wore a blue suit with an orchid in her lapel, and she waved a pair of reading glasses as she talked. "Good evening. I want to start off by thanking you all for being here and for your dedication..."

Gabriel tuned out the rest, listening for updates on the receiver and hearing nothing.

As she droned on, Mrs. Holsted pointed her glasses at a long table stacked with all kinds of stuff—bike helmets, picture frames, multicolored glass lamps, and stacks and stacks of manila envelopes. The envelopes held certificates for stuff that was too big or impractical to drag inside, or services donated by local merchants.

"Let's begin with services." Mrs. Holsted picked up an envelope and read the front. "We have an offer of a semester of swim lessons, any level, from Emler Swim Studio of Santa Marta."

"No, thank you," Peter moaned next to Gabriel. Marine-navigation-mad Peter was, incredibly, afraid of actual water. He hated swimming, and his throat would close up if he even tried to drink water.

Which was kind of amazing when Gabriel considered what they regularly went through together.

Peter looked at a printout his mom had fished out of her purse. "I want to bid on the snowboard."

"Snowboard?" Peter's mom scrunched up her eyebrows. "We don't have mountains."

"A guy can dream."

Gabriel scanned the room and the various corridors leading away to the exhibits. He saw a sign that read SHARKS off to the left. "I'm gonna go check out the sharks."

Peter shrugged like he wanted to go with him, but the

15

snowboard was coming up soon and so he gave him a thumbs-up instead.

"If your folks show, I want to say hi," Ms. Kosydar whispered as Gabriel left them.

In his ear, the coast guard voices rattled on.

"*Sqrrk.* We're out of warning buoys—can we call Santa Barbara and get some…"

He stopped and touched his ear to listen for a moment. Apparently the coast guard was running out of warning buoys for all the huge containers that had fallen into the water. Not something he could help with.

Gabriel paid more attention to the voices in his ear than where he was walking and collided with someone. He stepped sideways, headed for the shark exhibit, when a heavy hand on his shoulder whipped him around.

"Hey!" Larry Fife, an enormous eighth grader whose voice cracked painfully, pushed him back. Gabriel kept his balance.

"Sorry." Gabriel backed away.

"Whatsamatter, ET, the mother ship bothering you again?" Larry put his own hand to his own ear and made his eyes wide. "What's that? You want me to come home?"

"I said I was sorry," Gabriel tried again.

Larry, not as stupid as he appeared, had noticed Gabriel listening to the receiver several times at school. Gabriel usually tried to be more careful around other people, but with so much activity tonight he had gotten distracted. Gabriel cursed himself and vowed to keep from putting his hand to his ear when he was listening. The gesture was automatic, but it didn't help him blend in.

A goateed man nearby wearing a black suit cleared his throat loudly, and Larry slunk back to him. Gabriel took that opportunity to move on as he heard the man saying, "What have I told you? These people aren't worth it."

Nice. Listening to the coast guard drone on in his ear, Gabriel headed into the shark exhibit.

He found two great white sharks swimming in a relentless figure eight, as if patrolling the water as partners, one sweeping in right before Gabriel's eyes only to rush away, the second arriving just as the other had left. Two inches of Plexiglas separated the domain of the sharks and the darkened room where Gabriel stood watching them.

Gabriel heard a scuffling sound behind him and turned to see a line of chairs along the black-painted wall across from the tank. After a moment his eyes adjusted and he saw her: a little girl hiding underneath one of the chairs.

"Next up, a massage, two hours, offered by...," Mrs. Holsted said in the next room.

Gabriel approached the line of chairs and crouched, resting a hand on the front of one leather seat. "What are you doing down here?" he asked with a chuckle.

"I'm afraid of them." The girl peered out from under the leather seat, her body pressed back against the wall.

"Afraid of what?" Gabriel stayed crouched and followed

her saucer-wide eyes toward the tank, where one of the sharks circled again. "Oh, *them?*"

She nodded.

"What's your name?"

"Molly."

"I'm Gabriel. Where are your parents?"

"They're in there with my sister." Molly nodded toward the larger room where the parents and students were gathered. He figured her for about eight.

"Do I hear seventy-five?" Gabriel heard Mrs. Holsted again. "A massage makes a fine holiday gift, and at seventy-five..."

"Oh. Well, I could stand guard while you run back, but... you don't have to be afraid of these guys." Gabriel stood, walking over to the tank. He put his hand on the glass. "They're my friends."

"They *eat* people."

He smiled. "Where'd you hear that?"

"Taylor Cartwright had a sleepover and we watched *Jaws*."

Ahhh. Gabriel gave her a serious look. "Yeah, I saw that, too. That was pretty scary." *A little too scary for her age*, he thought, but then what did he know? His mom hadn't really approved of scary movies, though he and his sister had been into a lot of mythology stuff, and that could get gruesome.

"What do you mean they're your friends?"

Gabriel stepped back and scanned the tank until he saw a gold plaque that read: DINO AND GRACIE, RESCUED AND TEMPORARILY HOUSED THANKS TO THE SUPPORT OF ANONYMOUS DONORS.

Anonymous. He thought about the morning he'd had to sneak away from school to untangle Dino and Gracie from a tuna net then hand them off to someone who could see to it that they'd be taken care of. That was a good day, the kind of day that made him forget that he was here alone. Because how could you feel alone when there was a mission to complete? When it was done, Gabriel had swum away and returned to school. It was all...

Anonymous. No one.

There was another, older word for *no one*.

Nemo.

Gabriel gestured to Molly to come out. The smaller shark—only by a few inches—swam by. "Well, that one, the smaller one? That's Dino. There he goes. And this...is Gracie."

Molly crawled out from under the bank of chairs and came a few steps closer.

He continued, "These two sharks are *rescues*. That means they were injured in the ocean and the aquarium is giving them a place to live until they're better. And in the meantime you get to see them."

"But in *Jaws*…" Molly had stepped out to stand next to Gabriel.

"Do you eat fish?"

"Sure."

"That's what sharks eat. Mostly. Fish. Dolphins. They're not much interested in people." That wasn't entirely true, not if people got unlucky or stupid, but generally sharks were more interested in things that didn't intimidate them, and a human could be pretty intimidating.

Molly stared at him. "But they *could*, you mean. You're not sure."

She had him there. "Nothing's ever sure." Gabriel sighed. "I wouldn't want to lie to you."

"Molly!" A high voice called from the entrance to the shark exhibit. Gabriel turned to see Misty Jensen hurrying toward them, relief showing across her face.

He smiled wide. He had basically one other friend besides Peter, and that was Misty. "This is *your* sister?"

"We had no idea where you were!" Misty looked stern for a second and then melted as she hugged Molly. Then she addressed Gabriel, and her expression hardened ever so slightly again. "You couldn't bring her back where everyone else is?" She pushed back the bushy brown curls that insisted on falling over her face even when she tied them all back.

Gabriel spread his hands. "Well, she was asking about sharks."

Misty winced. "She's afraid of sharks, Gabe."

"Gabriel says sometimes they eat people. Like in *Jaws*!"

Misty's wince turned into a glare. "Did you tell her that sharks *eat* people?"

"*No*…maybe?" Gabriel blinked. "I was just *standing* here."

"There you are!" A woman spoke, and now two adults that Gabriel took to be Misty and Molly's parents came in. Both were dressed smartly in casual slacks and short-sleeved shirts that showed off what Gabriel had to admit were some pretty impressive physiques. He had only heard about them before. He had spent countless hours with Misty, but she had somehow maneuvered things so that he had never actually met her parents.

But oh, she worshipped them. Misty had told him that her parents were both retired from the air force. She said they lived *with purpose*, getting up at five in the morning to run and working out every afternoon. Truthfully, except for her longer hair, Misty was a dead ringer for her mom, down to the tan slacks.

"I was hiding from the sharks," Molly told her mom.

"Yeah." Misty jerked her thumb at Gabriel. "And then Bill Nye here started lecturing to her about how they eat people, apparently."

"She asked me…" Gabriel turned to her parents. "I'm Gabriel. And really, I don't lecture."

"He lectures all the time."

Gabriel turned to his friend. "No, no, see, this is a cool thing. It's really important to answer people when they ask questions, because that's when the brain is most engaged. All the neurons start lighting up. It's amazing! Actual physical changes occur, just because of a question."

She waved her arm. "See?"

Misty's parents extended their hands one at a time, and Gabriel shook them awkwardly. All these rituals. They'd rarely had visitors at home before his folks had sent him here. He always felt like he was pretending to know how to act. He was sure his hands were clammy.

Misty's mom looked him up and down. "We've heard of you. You're in the..."

"Marine research club?" Mr. Jensen tried to remember. "You do a lot of group excursions, right?"

Misty shot Gabriel a look that told him to go with it, and Gabriel obeyed. "Yep."

"Are your parents here?" Ms. Jensen asked. "We'd love to meet them."

"They're around somewhere." Which was true if you figured *somewhere* wasn't necessarily close by and included the bottom of the ocean.

The receiver in his ear burst to life with a woman's voice: "Mayday! Mayday! Pleasure vessel *Dandelion* requesting assistance. We have had a fire and are taking on water, requesting assistance at—" followed by a stream of numbers that were the coordinates for the woman's location.

Gabriel froze. Misty's mom was saying something, but he wasn't hearing it. He stared into space as he listened for a response.

Come on, guys, he thought. *Answer.*

"Excuse me." Gabriel took out his phone and started a note to himself. "I have to…" He stopped talking and typed the coordinates before he forgot them. Gabriel glanced up at Misty and her parents. "I was supposed to text… them. My parents. They may have gone to the wrong place." He babbled nonsense as he backed out of the exhibit. "I just realized. Uh, thanks."

As he hurried into the main room, he realized he never ended the conversation with the usual "nice to meet you." Whoops.

In the main room he tried his best to stick to the wall as he listened intently again.

"Come on, guys," he whispered.

The coast guard did not answer. Gabriel waited for the Mayday to come again.

Instead another voice came back: "*Sqrrk.* Can someone tell Santa Barbara we know they have at least thirty buoys? I mean, I'll get in a pickup and go get three of them right now."

This was followed by a lot of cross-traffic and laughing. It was as if the other call, the distress call, had never gone through.

Gabriel stared at the crowd and kept listening as the reality sank in. Incredible. The droning about the mess with the container vessel went on, and no one mentioned or responded to the call for help. The Mayday did not come again, and it was as if it had never happened.

There was a distress call, and the coast guard had missed it. No one knew that somewhere out there, someone was in trouble.

Except him. Gabriel Nemo had heard it.

When Gabriel was nine years old, his mother had taught him about cascading events, how tiny decisions and accidents can lead to large results, even catastrophes. Somewhere out there, at the spot described by the numbers Gabriel had just tapped out, a ship was in an emergency.

He had gotten his wish. Something terrible had happened.

Gabriel opened a new text on his phone and tapped a message to a group called CREW. He heard it *whoosh* away as he scanned the room for Peter.

Peter was standing with his mom right where Gabriel had left them, and Gabriel did his best to look only mildly excited as he tapped Peter on the shoulder.

"Hang on, the snowboard is next." Peter waved him off. Just then Peter's phone buzzed and he pulled it out of his pocket. Knowing it was the same text he had sent to Misty, Gabriel peered over Peter's shoulder to see the one-word message flash as a notification: OBSCURE.

Peter looked back furtively. "Are you sure—*now?*"

"Yes."

"Isn't there anybody…"

"There isn't. I'll fill you in once we get out of here."

"But I've got my mom. And what about Misty?"

"She's surrounded." Gabriel put on what he sincerely hoped was his best smile. "Ms. Kosydar? I'm totally sorry, but my dad just texted me to remind me that he's preparing this amazing, uh, kelp…dish." This wasn't far from likely. The Nemos were all about kelp. "Anyway, I have to go, but Peter is invited." He pointed at Peter as though she might not be sure who that was. "Dad, uh, said we could watch some movies and, you know, stay up late." He laid it on thick, knowing the clock was ticking.

They both waited expectantly.

"Well, I guess we don't both have to be here," she said.

"Great!" Having been given an out, Peter seemed determined not to wait around. He urged Gabriel on and they started running.

"But how will you get there?" she asked.

"We'll order a car!" Gabriel shouted, waving his phone. He brought up the app as they ran.

"Be very polite!" Ms. Kosydar called, but by that time they were out the door.

"How did you get here earlier?" Peter asked as they ran down the front steps to the curb.

"My bike, but it'll be fine." This was true. Anyone tampering with a Nemotech lock was going to get a zap a lot like that of Peter's imaginary jellyfish.

For a moment they stood at the edge of Ocean Highway, which was still thick with traffic at 7 P.M. Gabriel's address, a tiny wooden house on the cliffs of Santa Marta, was just a few miles up the highway.

"How long till your mom gets suspicious, do you think?" Gabriel asked.

"Could be a while."

Their driver was just pulling up as they heard another voice from behind them.

"You two could've waited for me," came the voice of Misty Jensen. Peter opened the car door and Misty slid in.

Peter laughed. "You got away! Gabe said you were surrounded."

She smirked. "What? You didn't think I was gonna miss this."

2

ON OCEAN HIGHWAY in Santa Marta, California, Gabriel's little wooden house lay silent as he, Peter, and Misty burst from the car at the curb and ran up the path. The dilapidated gate and door swung open as each sensed Gabriel drawing near.

Once safely inside, they kept moving but finally discussed what they had dared not let their driver overhear.

"Why isn't the coast guard taking this?" Peter asked. The house was so narrow that they could see out one window to the street and out the other straight over the cliff behind Gabriel's house to the Pacific Ocean, as calm as its name.

"They missed it, I guess." Gabriel and his friends moved into the living room. "There's an accident with a container vessel a few miles offshore. The radio has been crazy all afternoon."

"How long ago did you hear this distress call?" Misty asked as she reached the ratty old recliner in the living room, shoved it aside, and stepped on a tile in the floor.

"It came through while we were talking with your parents, so ... ten minutes at least." A trapdoor opened, and the three peered down to see lapping black water and a dark, round hatch, whose rivets shone in the dim light with mother-of-pearl inlays, sticking up above the waves eighty feet below.

Gabriel's house rested on a sturdy latticework frame crafted out of a polymer that Gabriel's family had been perfecting since before his father was born. The frame allowed the house itself to hang out over the rocky cliff. The beach at the bottom had been dug out when this house—really just a facade with a kitchen and some furniture—was built. A metal ladder extended all the way down, interrupted occasionally by platforms and walkways to allow passage to a variety of equipment and data-collection tools. The whole structure glowed with its own light, a phosphorous blue-green paint devised by Gabriel's ancestors, and was hidden on the other side by an artificial cliff. From the water, an observer would see only weeds where the house ended and rock all the way down.

With his crew close behind, Gabriel put his feet on

either side of the ladder and slid down, away from a home that was barely a home at all and toward a better one.

~~~

Stepping onto the command bridge of the hidden submarine, Gabriel tapped the coordinates of the distress call into a touchpad embedded in a polished-coral panel and looked up at the enormous view screen currently showing a map of the Pacific coastline. Noting the blinking green spot, he turned his attention back to the pad, going through the pre-launch checklist.

"Still no more Maydays?" Misty called out as she bounded down the ladder and disappeared into a small changing room Gabriel had designed and installed for her when she joined the crew.

"Nothing since the first one." Gabriel touched a button. Electrical cells at maximum. No surprise there. They hadn't taken the *Obscure* out in two weeks, and he'd been careful to recharge the seaweed-conversion alternators before they docked.

Peter moved quickly to his own panel and put an earpiece in as he glanced up at the large map. "That's only about forty miles out. Are you sure it's safe?"

"It's what we do, Peter. We'll handle it. It's up to us."

"But you could be seen."

"We'll…handle it." Gabriel waved his hand.

Peter reached under the panel and grabbed a green

wet suit, then hurriedly tore off his shirt and pants. "Heads up!" Peter shouted. "Changing."

"Okay," Misty called. "Thanks for the warning."

"You check the engines?"

"Yes." Gabriel pulled on his own wet suit and nodded at Peter. "I have a protective suit for you, too. You never know what might get scratched up."

Peter rolled his eyes and settled back in his seat. "Yeah, sure. Next time." He flipped a few more switches. "I hope you know I was planning to go home and watch a *Johnny Mullet* marathon after the auction."

"How can you watch those things?" Gabriel asked, zipping up the front of the wet suit.

"Your real question *should* be how I can pass it up to spend time in a tin can with *you*." Peter tapped a button. "Engines engaged. And anyway, you know I'm not gonna get scratched up because I never leave the boat."

Gabriel held up his hands. "Preparation is all I'm saying."

But Peter was generally right. The submarine didn't trigger Peter, in the same way that being up in a plane might not bother those who were afraid of heights. But with his fear of water, Peter would not go on any excursion outside the *Obscure*.

The floor began to vibrate slightly, humming as the engines came online.

"Why were you with the sharks, anyway? Wasn't there

anything you wanted to bid on?" Misty called from her changing room.

"I think he just got bored," Peter said.

"I don't get bored," Gabriel insisted, tapping buttons. He might get homesick and lonely, but never bored. He had all the brilliance of the sea to entertain him and vessels in distress to rescue. Plus tonight he'd actually made an effort to show up at an event. Who could be bored with all that?

Right?

"What kind of ship is it?" Misty asked from her changing room.

Gabriel remembered. "It's a pleasure vessel called the *Dandelion.*"

"Oh yeah! My cousin had a wedding reception on that."

Gabriel thought about the implications of a boat used for wedding receptions. Party barge, then. Passengers, some drinking, possibly kids and babies. Possibly people who couldn't swim.

Misty continued. "And by the way, I'm the one who's supposed to monitor communications."

"I can get you a Nemotech receiver if you really want one, but the hard part is ignoring it." Gabriel found his seat and grabbed a bottle of soda out of a small refrigerator he kept underneath a hatch next to the captain's chair. The soda was of his family's own recipe, made of sweetened kelp.

Peter made a gagging sound. "You want to talk about taste—I can't believe you drink that stuff."

"We like kelp." Gabriel shrugged.

The whole bridge, from its bulkheads to the frames of its hatches and portholes, shone with mother-of-pearl and the dark, mysterious metal crafted by the Nemos for all their ships. It made Gabriel feel warm inside. This was what he needed to be doing. He should have been sorry to take his friends away on a Friday, but surely a rescue mission would beat... whatever it was people did when they didn't have *this*.

Because that's what you're telling yourself to push away the truth, came an unwanted voice inside him. *That you are bored, and lonely, and who needs you and your—*

"Misty, what did you tell your parents, anyway?" Gabriel called.

"I said I forgot we had a night rescue-swimming practice that I couldn't be late for," came her reply.

Misty competed on the middle school swim team and had nearly completed her certification in water rescue and emergency response. The certification was part of a checklist that Misty had put together when she was eleven years old, a list that currently filled several pages in a notebook she decorated in strange, fractured swirls. The list included, among other things, water rescue, rock climbing, conversational Chinese, negotiations, shooting, archery, and public speaking. She had already made her way through about a quarter of the original list, so she kept adding more things to it. She had a rough term for what she wanted to be—an "action girl." As far as Gabriel could tell, she was trying to become a superhero.

"Won't they be...um...worried or something?" Gabriel asked.

Misty's laugh sounded from the other room. "Hey, Peter, listen to Gabriel ask about parents like they're some alien race he's unfamiliar with. But no, you're lucky. I just gotta be home by ten."

"Speaking of parents...my mom was leaning kind of hard on wanting to meet yours," Peter said from across the bridge.

"What?" Gabriel asked.

"My mom," Peter repeated, "still wants to meet your parents."

"My parents do, too!" Misty came out wearing a red diving suit and dropped into a swivel chair in front of a bank of communications and sonar equipment that would have been bewildering to anyone but her or Gabriel, who had de-signed it. "Especially now that you scared my sister half to death with your Shark Week talk."

"Not gonna happen unless they want to go to the bottom of the ocean." That was true. His father rarely set foot on land, certainly not in Gabriel's memory. And his mom

33

had adopted the same rule when she'd married his dad. "Let's focus, okay?"

"Right, right. So those are the coordinates? Scanning now." Misty ran her eyes over the screen. "Seriously, though, I don't know how long we can go on like this."

"It's worked for—"

"Six months," Misty answered, "and I'm glad the experiment is going well, but how much longer is *Hey, I have to run to a sudden swim practice* really a viable—"

"Can we pl—"

Peter interrupted. "Rescue first, folks. Gabriel, I got a craft on radar about forty miles east-southeast of here, standing still. Could be the one."

"All right, then." Gabriel smiled. Misty and Peter weren't like anyone else. He was lucky to have them in his life. They knew how to live *obscure*.

I am willing to live obscure. That was what *he*, Gabriel's ancestor, technically his great-great-great-grandfather, had proclaimed. To live in service to the sea and count all else as distraction. That was what drove Gabriel forward, what pushed away the loneliness and the doubt.

Peter and Misty were the two people who had caught a glimpse of that creed and seized it.

No matter how they might complain, Gabriel could count on them. "Take us out, Peter."

"Aye, aye, Captain."

3

THIRTY-EIGHT MILES FROM shore, the dinner ship *Dandelion* was in trouble. Panicked passengers had gathered hopelessly on the deck when the *Obscure*, sixty-five feet long and looking like a strange, tapered alien creature from the deep, broke the surface and approached.

Gabriel and Misty appeared on a catwalklike platform above the water as floodlights mounted on the nose and tail of the *Obscure* shone toward the boat.

All around them the black waves reflected moonlight and fire.

"Ahoy!" Gabriel cried through a bullhorn shaped like a conch shell. He had fashioned the bullhorn himself. He liked to think that the original Captain Nemo, who took energy from the sea and moved through it like a natural part of it, would approve of how Gabriel had tried to bring that respect for the sea to every detail.

"Ahoy there! We're going to come alongside! Please try to keep clear."

Misty leaned on the mother-of-pearl-inlaid iron bars of the platform at the top of the *Obscure*. "Oh, she's in bad shape." The *Dandelion* was beginning to dip its deck close to the water. There was still a fire spewing out of one of the forward hatches from what Gabriel assumed was the kitchen.

Gabriel thumbed the joystick and D-pad on the silvery controller in his hand, guiding the *Obscure* closer. For close-up positioning like this, he couldn't ask Peter down in the bridge to move the entire sub a few yards forward and back by voice commands only. Better to do it by sight, so he'd worked with his family to perfect the controller. The truth was, though, this was only the third time he'd used it outside of testing.

When he was at last satisfied that the two vessels were perfectly parallel, Gabriel tapped a button and felt a throb in the deck plates as satellite-guided stabilizer rotors kicked in to hold the *Obscure* in place. "Plank."

Misty kicked a lever near her foot, and a long metal walkway began to unroll and fasten itself together as it went. Lined with floatation material, it bobbed on the water as it extended out about twenty feet. Gabriel watched as a woman treading water grabbed onto it.

"Where's the captain?" Gabriel shouted, dropping the bullhorn now that they were closer.

Gabriel heard the sound of a fire extinguisher and saw a woman in a uniform with gold epaulettes wielding it. The woman called, "Someone! Grab that plank and lift it onto the deck!" She looked out to the *Obscure*, squinting as if to make out Gabriel's form. "I'm the captain."

"How many on board?"

"We're twenty-three souls. Can you take that many?"

One of the passengers had already placed the plank onto the sinking vessel, and passengers began to scramble across. As they climbed onto the submarine, Misty pointed down through the open hatch toward the ladder. Gabriel heard her saying, "Be careful, watch your head, take a seat in the long room through the hatch."

"We can take sixty-four if we need to." The *Dandelion* was taking on water fast.

One by one the passengers came aboard, stumbling along the plank and then down the hatch. Gabriel thanked the forces of all oceanic chaos that there was no one who needed carrying.

The captain of the *Dandelion* waited until the last person was on the platform before she came across. When she drew close she saw Gabriel clearly. She furrowed her brow as if confused. "You're a kid."

"Well, the coast guard had a thing."

She looked at the *Obscure*. "What in the world is this... vessel?"

Gabriel smiled. "This is my home."

As Gabriel retracted the plank, a massive explosion of bubbles burst from the *Dandelion* as the cabin met the water. He heard the fire in the front hiss out as the electric lights flickered and died. Then, lit only by the moon and the *Obscure*'s floodlights, the boat shifted sideways like a dolphin turning over to dive. In a moment, the last panels of white-washed wood slipped under and out of sight.

Amazing how fast they go at the last moment.

Down below, inside the *Obscure*, a woman screamed. "Jacob! Jacob! Where's my son?"

Gabriel came down the ladder behind the captain of the *Dandelion* into the long room of benches where the passengers were buckling themselves in. Little portholes along the wall let in light from the outside hull, lighting up fish and speckles of debris. Many of the passengers craned their necks to look out, and on the port side, the *Dandelion* dropped past like a ghost in the darkness.

Pacing up and down the length of the room, a woman was visibly agitated.

Gabriel asked, "What is it?"

Misty ran up to him. "A boy. There was a little boy. He's *missing*."

"Are you sure?"

"Am I *sure*?" the woman snarled. "He's not *here*."

"Okay." Gabriel surveyed the passengers anyway, looking for any sign of someone hiding. *People under stress don't have full use of their eyes. Their field of vision narrows and the light gets weird.* Tunnel vision, his mother had called it. *People in a panic miss things.*

And more: They're high on adrenaline. Don't let it infect you, because one of you has to be the one who's not infected.

Gabriel didn't see anyone. *Oh, no.*

The captain put her arms on the woman's shoulders and looked her in the eyes. "Mrs. McNally, where was he?"

"I think..." Mrs. McNally shook her hands as if to clear her head. "I think he was in the bathroom."

"How old is he?" Gabriel asked.

"Jacob is seven." Her voice was choked with uncontrollable sobs.

Misty stared at Gabriel, clearly thinking the same thing he was. Gabriel felt the blood drain from his face. "That boat just sank," he whispered.

Think. Was it possible? Could someone still be alive...?

He looked at Mrs. McNally. Only one way to find out. Gabriel slapped a button on a com panel. "Peter, fill the tanks, tilt hydroplane levers. *Dive.*"

"Aye, aye," came the answer, and in the walls Gabriel heard a rushing sound, water coming into the double hull.

"Everyone grab on," Gabriel ordered as the *Obscure*

began to tilt forward. "Remain seated. There are seat belts—I urge you to use them."

"What are you doing?" asked the captain of the *Dandelion*.

Gabriel ran forward and distinctly downhill through the next hatch. "I'm going after your boat."

Gabriel and Misty shot into the bridge, and they saw the *Dandelion* racing ahead of them, a great gray, fire-blackened hulk that filled the view screen of the bridge as it sank. "Catch it!"

Peter looked back. "Gabriel, what are you talking about?"

"There's a kid on board. There may still be time to save him," Gabriel replied, gripping the console.

"How, alive how?" Peter demanded.

"There could be an air pocket," Gabriel reasoned.

"If there is then it will burst before the ship hits the bottom."

"Then we need to *catch* it, Peter."

Peter wasn't having it. "It's heavier than us. It's sinking faster than we can move."

Gabriel thought. He wasn't going to give up that easily. "Engines."

"I'm using them."

"Try something else, then," Misty demanded. "We have to save him, and we're running out of time."

"We could pull it back with the winch." Gabriel tapped a screen furiously as he brought up the control panel for the towing cables. While the harpoons weren't often used, the heavy cables located on the fore and aft sides of the sub had assisted in more than one rescue mission. He glanced at Peter and Misty. "What do you think?"

Misty nodded. "It'll take a lucky shot, but it might work."

"Are you two insane?" Peter shook his head in disbelief. "Gabriel, you've already gotten twenty-something people off a sinking ship. If you use the cables to grab onto that boat, it will drag us to the bottom of the ocean."

"It won't," Gabriel insisted. "Not if we're moving in reverse, pulling back on it."

"It's full of water!" Peter shot back. "That thing is a hundred tons if it's an ounce; it is as *heavy* as we are and it's sinking like a *stone*, Gabe. It's ballast, it's dead weight, it's too much, and it will drag us down."

"We can handle depths way deeper than this."

"Not with that kind of stress on our prow. It'll weaken the whole frame and make us susceptible to rupture. Doing this could kill *everyone*."

Misty didn't say another word, but he could read her thoughts on her face.

The argument was taking time they didn't have. He had a split second to make a decision. His mother had been walking Gabriel through situations like this since before he could walk. He felt the anxiety drain out as he found a distant spot on which to concentrate his mind.

Yeah.

He made his voice calm and firm. "Cable it."

Peter didn't protest again. That was their way. *Debate with me. Challenge me. But when we choose a course, debate is done.* "Cables away."

Gabriel heard a distant *shunk* and watched as two long, silvery cables with harpoon tips shot out from below the prow of the *Obscure*.

It took three seconds.

Wham. The harpoons stuck in the hide of the falling vessel. Immediately Gabriel was thrown off balance as the *Obscure* thrust forward and down, picking up speed and sinking.

"Blow all ballast tanks. Make us into a balloon, Peter." They had to get lighter, quickly, and start heading up toward the surface. "Reverse engines full. Drag it up with us."

Peter pulled back on the joystick at his console, and Gabriel could see it was slow going. The weight was fighting with him. "Reverse engines full. You will note that we are still sinking."

"*Just*"—Gabriel wrung his hands—"bear with me, okay?" He turned to Misty. "Come on, we're going out."

"DPVs?"

"Aye."

Gabriel and Misty ran uphill, up the long center of the *Obscure*, pushing past the passengers and the agonized mother. The captain of the *Dandelion* called out, "You need help?"

As Misty unlocked the rear hatch, Gabriel turned back. "Just keep everybody calm. We're working on it."

"With what?"

"Driver propulsion vehicles," Misty answered. "We're gonna turn ourselves into submarines."

Misty slammed the hatch shut behind them as Gabriel started filling the dive room, turning a wheel that was, like everything else, inlaid with shells. The dive room was about eight feet wide and shaped like a pinecone turned on its side. As the room filled with water, Gabriel opened a locker and drew out devices that looked like thick green markers. He handed the first one to Misty and kept the other for himself, hooking it to his mask so he couldn't lose it. Short-term rebreathers.

Nemotech, of course.

Peter came over the intercom when the water was up to Gabriel's chest. "Gabriel, we've stopped sinking."

"Good!" Gabriel shouted. He and Misty pulled on diving masks. Thumbs-up.

Peter sounded unsure. "But . . . we don't have long."

"Why?"

"I'm doing everything I can—the ballast tanks are empty, the engines are on full reverse—but we are going to burn them out if we keep straining like this."

Gabriel looked around him, feeling the tug of the *Obscure* against itself. "How long?"

"I give it ten minutes."

43

Misty and Gabriel locked eyes through their diving masks. The kid—any kid on that boat—probably wouldn't even last that long. It might be too late already. They didn't say this, but Gabriel knew they were both thinking it. They gave each other the thumbs-up sign again as the water reached the ceiling.

The irislike hatch in the floor opened silently, and Gabriel inhaled through the rebreather and peered into the open ocean below.

4

TEN MINUTES, GABRIEL reminded himself, then quickly set a timer on his wristband. Ten minutes, that was all Peter could give them.

Misty went first, sinking down out of the submarine, and Gabriel didn't even wait the usual nine seconds before following. He nearly hit her on the head as he dropped away from the ship, and she opened her hands in a gesture that said, *Watch it.*

They swam together under the hull of the *Obscure*, the underhull lamps lighting their way. Beyond the sound of his breath, Gabriel could hear the high-pitched whine of the engines. Peter was right: The cables attached to the dead *Dandelion* were tugging, and the *Obscure* could barely stand the strain.

Gabriel kept a lot of useful stuff tethered to the bottom of the *Obscure*. As he and Misty swam along the sixty-five-foot hull, they passed a two-person minisub the size of a small car and a motorcyclelike "manned torpedo" called a Katana, until they arrived at what he was looking for: a pair of personal DPVs. They were like rugged boogie boards with propellers. The rider grabbed hold and *went*.

Gabriel pulled at the lever that held the metal straps around the DPV in place and it dropped, remaining slightly buoyant. He flipped a switch near the front and felt it yank in his hands. He held on to the black, rubberized handles on the sides and sped down past the *Obscure*'s nose along one of the cables.

He looked briefly over his shoulder to see Misty behind him, like a red porpoise, her long legs fluttering in the water as she guided her own DPV.

"Can you hear me?" Gabriel spoke into the mic in the rebreather mouthpiece. He looked at his watch. *Tick tick tick.*

"Five by five." Misty's voice sounded in his mask. "Loud and clear."

A loud *pop* shot through the water. *Oh, no.* Gabriel sucked in a breath as the cable they were flying along made several more alarming, wobbly metal sounds. If it snapped, they'd lose the boat—and the little boy trapped inside—for good.

"We gotta hurry." They reached the edge of the cable, and Gabriel brought his feet smack against the hull of the

Dandelion. It took him a moment to get oriented. The vessel was almost completely upside down.

They swam over the upside-down bottom of the vessel looking for a way inside.

"There's the hole." Misty pointed out a section of the wooden hull that had blown out, the boards separated and pushed out by some explosion in the engine. It looked as though someone had punched the boards with a giant hammer. Engines could fly apart and do that. As he swam on, Gabriel was beginning to understand the course of events—some kind of kitchen fire, a spreading fire, an exploding engine, then a breached hull.

But the explosion hadn't been enough to cause a hole they could swim in through, so they moved on quickly. They would have to go up into the hull from the main entrance. Within moments they were swimming down toward the door that earlier had belched smoke and flame.

"We have six minutes left. Let's clip the DPVs here." Gabriel put up his hand to the side of the doorway as he edged through, catching a glimpse of his wristband receiver. "There's not enough room inside." He touched a button on his mask and a line of tiny LEDs lit up, casting light in front of them. Misty did the same, doubling the visibility in the darkened space.

The bridge was awash in half-burnt papers and Coke cans, along with other varied flotsam and jetsam left behind by the tourists. Within a moment they had found the stairwell that had been the way belowdecks but that now was an upside-down stairway going up.

"The head should be toward the front of this level. Gabe, do you think it could be airtight?" *Head* was the nautical term for bathroom, though chances were a civilian vessel like the *Dandelion* would simply call it a bathroom.

"On a pleasure craft like this?" Gabriel shook his head. "Seems unlikely. Best we could hope for is trapped air." Sometimes when a ship turned over, air could fill parts of the deck. If Jacob were lucky enough to be in one, he might still be breathing. Even if he wasn't, Gabriel thought, they still needed to get him. People could be revived after drowning if the rescuer moved fast enough. Sometimes.

None of that would matter if the *Dandelion* fell apart before they reached him.

They swam up the stairs to reach a corridor lined with brown wooden paneling. The carpet on the floor above Gabriel's head shimmied as he swam under it.

Gabriel signaled to turn as they reached a new corridor. "You feel a slight rise here?"

"Yes. We're going up a little."

Gabriel's eye caught a strange shimmer in the water as they turned, and he raced forward. "Air!" In a moment his head splashed up out of the water. He let his rebreather drop and dangle at his chin as Misty surfaced as well.

The space between the water's surface and the carpet above them was about two feet. They paddled, moving down the corridor. Then they heard it—muffled cries coming from behind one of the doors.

Misty swam ahead and stopped at the plywood door. "Here." Gabriel dipped his head under and saw a plastic plaque on the door that read MEN.

Gabriel came up beside her and beat on the door. "Hey! Hey! Anybody in there!"

A voice, small and fragile, cried out. "Hello?"

"Are you Jacob?" Gabriel called.

"Yes!"

Water splashed around Gabriel's head as the walls and decks around them groaned heavily. A strip of wood siding cracked and popped free, falling past his head. The boat was starting to crumple. "We're gonna get you out of here, okay? Can you open the door?"

"I can't," the voice came back. They heard splashing. "I'm hanging on to the toilet bowl. It's . . . on the ceiling."

"That's . . . that's good!" Gabriel looked back at Misty and shouted to Jacob again. "Can you reach the doorknob?"

"I can't! It's underwater!"

Misty dove and Gabriel saw her go around him, trying the doorknob. She splashed up again. "It's locked. We're running out of time, Gabe. This boat is going to tear apart."

He looked at his wristband. "We have four minutes." Gabriel tried again, shouting at the upside-down door. "Can you let go, swim down, and turn the knob?"

"No!" came the answer. "I want to go home!"

"I know, I . . ." Gabriel treaded water and looked back at Misty.

The boat shuddered as Gabriel heard a heavy crunch—*too* heavy. Most likely the keel, the central beam that ran along the bottom of the boat, had snapped. She might hold together after that. Might. But within moments one or all of these things were going to happen: The engines of the *Obscure* would burn out, causing it and the *Dandelion* to sink. Or the cables would break free and the *Dandelion*, again, would sink. Or the whole boat would fall apart and likely kill them in the process. Three options, all ending in death. They had to move quickly. "We've gotta get this door open." Gabriel looked around. "Find *anything.*"

They put in their rebreathers and plunged underwater again. Gabriel scanned along the corridor by the light of his headlamps. He saw pens, staplers.

Think.

He remembered the fire extinguisher the captain had used. There might be another. Or maybe he had time to swim back out to the upper deck and look for it. That *might* be heavy enough to break the lock. Except he'd have to swing it underwater, and that would make his blows slower, sluggish. Still.

Under the water, Gabriel saw Misty seize a fallen pen holder next to an overturned desk in the corridor. They both surfaced, and she held out two ballpoint pens. "What are you doing?"

"We don't have to break it down." She unscrewed the pens, discarding the useless pieces until she held out two steel ink-pen tubes.

Misty put on her rebreather again and dove toward the doorknob. Gabriel followed and watched her thrust the steel rods into the doorknob of the bathroom.

"Are you serious?" he asked through his mouthpiece.

"Not now, Gabe—"

After a moment she hissed in frustration, and then he heard her again. "'Kay. 'Kay."

It wasn't going to work. He was going to lose the boy and ruin the whole rescue because they couldn't get through an upside-down door. *Think*. Maybe he could kick it. If he got up and put his shoulders against the wall and his feet against the door. If he was tall enough to get leverage. *If, if, if.*

Then: "Got it." Misty backed up and turned the knob. Sure enough, she had picked the lock. *That* was cool.

They both surfaced in the bathroom. Right in front of them, Jacob McNally's face was as white as the porcelain toilet bowl he clung to.

"I'll take him." Gabriel propelled himself forward to grab Jacob, who instantly put his arms around the older boy's neck. Gabriel smoothly moved the Jacob's hands to his shoulders. He was accustomed to panicked swimmers grabbing his neck and was adept at redirecting them. Gabriel looked at Misty. "Hurry, go ahead of me—tell Peter to be ready to get out of here."

The hull of the boat shook as carpet broke free from above and more strips of paneling popped, one after the other, like fingers coming alive to grab them. Misty disappeared into the water. Gabriel looked back at Jacob, whose fingers dug fiercely into his wet suit. They had maybe a minute. Gabriel unclipped his rebreather and held it up. "I'm gonna give you this thing to put in your mouth and you breathe through it, okay?"

Jacob stared. Gabriel reached back and put the rebreather's strap around the boy's head, then brought the device to the boy's mouth. "Breathe, try it."

Jacob sucked in air.

"Okay. You breathe through that, and don't take it off." He looked into the other boy's eyes and tried, tried to push away every ounce of worry in his own. "My name is Gabriel. And we're gonna go under the water now, and there is absolutely . . . nothing . . . to be afraid of."

Jacob nodded.

Gabriel pictured the swim through the corridor, the stairs, out, two hundred yards or so to the *Obscure.*

Nothing to be afraid of. Sure.

He wouldn't be free-swimming—the DPV would help them move fast once they were free of the boat—but still, that was going to be, what, four minutes underwater?

Gabriel pictured countless mornings, looking up through shimmering water at his father at the edge of a pool, an enormous digital stopwatch displayed on a tiled wall behind him.

Learn and be able to do.

Pushing away the noises coming from the ship and the boy, Gabriel closed his eyes. He straightened his body, letting his rib cage stretch out. He took a deep breath, feeling air going deep into his lungs, and shut his mouth. Then he worked his cheeks in brief pumps, forcing oxygen down fistfuls at a time. Lung-packing, his father called it.

Ready. He hoped.

Gabriel plunged under the water with Jacob gripping his shoulders. He swam, kicking, trying to accommodate Jacob's weight, heading down, down and out.

Down the stairs. Out through broken windows. Gabriel felt the first crackling deep in his body of carbon dioxide acidifying in his blood, signaling his all-too-human brain to start trying to breathe. A signal he ignored as he grabbed the DPV and turned it on.

Gabriel and Jacob swept out and up, following the path of the groaning, churning cable.

His lungs burned and he pushed on, one hundred yards. Two.

By the time they reached the hull of the *Obscure*, the submarine was shaking so hard that it sounded ready to explode. Gabriel's lungs were ready to burst and he concentrated, one step at a time, one motion at a time. He had to do everything right: just *don't breathe.*

Gabriel pushed Jacob up through the dive porthole and followed. By the time they were both inside the dive room,

Gabriel's vision was filling with inky spots and he was losing the ability to move his arms. He looked past the growing shadows and slapped a seashell-shaped control, and the porthole swiveled shut. Water began to flow out and he pushed to the top, gasping as air plunged back into his lungs again.

Gabriel staggered in the puddle of water that remained as Jacob shook uncontrollably on the floor. The whole room was angled sideways due to the forward pitch of the sub, and Gabriel found it difficult to balance. He leaned on the wall and gasped again.

Yeah. Nothing to be afraid of.

Gabriel felt the shaking of the *Obscure* in the wall and remembered the danger he—and all those passengers—still faced. He pushed the intercom on the wall. "Peter!"

"Captain!"

Gabriel coughed. His vision was back, though. "Is Misty with you on the bridge?"

Misty's voice came on. "Just made it."

"Cut engines and cut cable and get us out of here."

"Aye—"

Idiot!

"Wait, no, belay that, belay!" *Where is your brain?* Gabriel slapped his forehead and snatched up Jacob, seating them both next to the door on a metal bench. Like the room, the bench leaned back, and they looked *up* at the tail of the sub.

As Gabriel grabbed safety restraints and clicked them in place, he spoke again. "Okay, *now*, Peter."

"Aye, aye."

Even inside the sub, Gabriel could hear the sharp crack as the cable was cut loose from the nose of the *Obscure*, and at once the submarine rose—*fast*, let loose like a stone from a slingshot. The thrust of the rising vessel threw them back against the wall as the *Obscure* pushed hungrily toward the surface.

Jacob started screaming.

Gabriel felt the weightlessness of the entire ship as the *Obscure* broke the surface. He could picture it: the long, mother-of-pearl plates with seashell ornamentations and shimmering lights erupting with a spectacular spray of ocean water, the whole submarine shooting up like a dancing whale.

Gabriel shouted, "Hang on!"

They slammed back onto the surface of the water, the *Obscure* shaking and sliding until it came to a rest in a steady, humming state, floating on the calm ocean.

For a moment, a brief moment his father would likely not have approved of, he thought: *We actually made it.*

Then Gabriel unclicked the belt and went to the hatch at the wall, opening it up to peer into the next room. He saw Misty running down the corridor toward them.

"Jacob!" Misty sounded out of breath. "Your mother wants to see you."

As she led Jacob away by the hand, Gabriel grinned at her. "You gotta tell me where you learned to pick locks."

～ン～

They dropped off the survivors of the lost *Dandelion* at the Santa Marta marina, on a distant jetty where the sounds of "Margaritaville" drifted on the night air from nearby restaurants. Gabriel only had one request, especially for the captain and Mrs. McNally: that they say *nothing* about who had come to their aid.

Gabriel didn't want the attention. "Promise me."

Because who had it been?

No one.

And with that, the *Obscure* slipped away once more.

5

GABRIEL BLINKED AWAKE at two in the morning to the sound of his cell phone buzzing. He shifted in the hammock strung across his room, still groggy, not sure what he had heard at first. The sounds of clanking sailboat lines on the marina drifted in from outside, and suddenly his phone buzzed again. He snatched it up from the nightstand next to his hammock.

The screen read: ANONYMOUS.

Gabriel hit a green button and held the phone up to his ear. "Hello?"

There was a whir, and then a fake, metallic voice rattled out a response.

"Four. Six. Oh. One. Two." And then, *click*.

Station 46012 was a great, yellow weather buoy ten miles off the coast of California. It belonged to NOAA, the National Oceanic and Atmospheric Administration, but Gabriel knew it wasn't the government that wanted to meet him there.

The cool water slid past Gabriel's body as he rode the Katana, a slender vehicle about the width and length of a motorcycle. Riding the Katana was like using a Jet Ski but underwater. Handlebars allowed for direction control while levers at the rider's feet controlled depth and speed. He loved it: The underwater motorbike was the coolest thing (besides a sixty-five-foot submarine) that his parents had ever given him.

Misty liked it, too, but of course Peter stayed as far away from it as possible.

On the Katana's control panel sonar screen, a pulsating orb came into view about a mile from his location. That would be the buoy. About time to lighten up. Gabriel sped another half mile and then adjusted the ballast lever with his heel. Water pushed out of the tanks, and he shot upward. Within moments he surfaced.

Waves lapped around Gabriel as he took the rebreather out of his mouth and let it dangle. The bright-yellow buoy looked like a twelve-foot-wide floating beaker—or a yellow genie bottle—bobbing on the water as Gabriel approached it. A light at the top of the beacon swiveled around, blinding him and then sweeping away, blinding and sweeping.

Gabriel circled the buoy slowly, glancing back to shore, where just over the horizon he could see the glow of Santa Marta. The buoy—one of twenty or so along California's shoreline that measured waves, wind, and pressure, constantly recording and sending information up to government satellites that scoured the data for weather patterns—clanked softly as it rocked. Because the buoys never moved and had numbered addresses, they made useful meeting spots.

A light under the water caught Gabriel's eye. He swiveled around to watch the light grow as it rose fast just a few yards away from his Katana.

Nerissa?

But it wasn't a personal craft. Instead, a metal pole, long and inlaid with silvery, incandescent organic material like the hull of every vessel in Gabriel's family, broke through the waves.

It was *another* buoy, this one smaller and not a kind recognized by any government agency. No sooner had the silvery bulb at the bottom surfaced than it began to hum.

A metal rod slid out from the top of the pole and extended, unfolding into an upside-down L. There were nozzles running along the pole, and as the pieces locked into place with a tiny *click*, water vapor began to spray from the nozzles.

"I need you to look at something for me," came a voice from behind him, and Gabriel gasped, nearly falling off his

Katana. He looked back and was nearly blinded by an illuminating beam shooting out from a second craft.

Someday, he vowed, she would not be able sneak up on him.

Behind the light he saw an uncertain image, part visible, part hidden in shadow, a teenage girl with thick hair wet and clumped around her shoulders. She dimmed her Katana's headlamp. Her eyes, large and black, her dusky skin: There was nothing about her that didn't spell *sister.*

"I knew it was you."

"I need you to look at this," she repeated, more urgent this time. "We don't have much time."

Gabriel had not seen his sister in nearly a year, and he was certain his parents had not either. Everyone in the family had to deal with the Nemo legacy. The original Captain Nemo, Gabriel's great-great-great-grandfather, who first devised the many principles that drove the technologies they used, had chosen a dark path of vengeance on governments he despised. Mom and Dad had rejected that path. Living and working in the Nemolab at the bottom of the ocean, they had chosen peace. Gabriel had chosen... whatever this life was now. A kind of quasi-peace, he guessed.

Nerissa Nemo, however, really was living up to Captain Nemo's darkest legacy. Nerissa used her vessel, the *Nebula,* to strike illegal whalers and anyone else she found to be disrespectful to the sea. At only eighteen years old, she was already a fugitive, wanted for the destruction of at least five vessels. Which was why Gabriel and his parents didn't get to see her much anymore. Not that he saw much of his parents, either. A few times a year. All part of the experiment.

How much was Nerissa risking coming to see him? She wouldn't be alone, regardless. Gabriel knew her own vessel lay somewhere within the range of the Katana she rode. Aboard the two-hundred-foot *Nebula*, a loyal crew waited with heavy weapons. He had heard her called the Joan of Arc of the Sea.

"Don't have much *time*?" Gabriel repeated. "What do you mean?"

"Just look at this."

Gabriel shook his head in confusion, and she pointed at the buoy she had sent ahead of her. On a "screen" made up of water vapor a few feet from where Gabriel sat, the light from Nerissa's Katana projected a grainy color image of high waves somewhere in the middle of the ocean. Thanks to the orange container boxes stacked at the bottom of the image, Gabriel knew he was looking at a shot taken from one of the vast multinational container vessels that crossed the Pacific constantly. Those containers were twenty feet long, the ships themselves enormous. Ocean spray crashed against the deck, and in the gray daylight, waves that dwarfed the giant ships chopped into the distance.

"This image was taken a month ago in the North Pacific

Gyre," Nerissa said. "Right where all the currents of the Pacific come together, smack-dab between California and Japan."

"I know where it is." Gabriel rolled his eyes. He'd studied it when he was five, just as she had.

"Okay, okay." Nerissa held up a hand. "Look at the shape in the water there, behind the big wave hitting the deck."

Gabriel heard a flicking sound as Nerissa turned on a laser pointer and circled a shadow that he had not yet noticed in the image. The shadow was below the surface, but large, boat-sized.

"Well, that's a whale."

"No." Nerissa clicked a button. The image advanced, and now something was coming out of the water, shiny, almost like glass. "Try again."

"What in..." Gabriel turned back to her, squinting to see her face. "Is it a sub?"

"Look closer." She clicked again.

In this image, the shape had surfaced and lay there on the waves. Gabriel felt a chill run through his body. It wasn't a ship or a sub, but a crumpled *airplane*, with its glass cockpit still intact, its propeller long gone. Red circles on each wing identified its make and purpose.

"That's a Japanese Zero Fighter." That was crazy. "From World War Two. Is it—Did someone outfit it with ballast tanks and make a sub out of it? I don't get this."

"What you don't see is something that the crewman who sent me these pictures told me. Those wings are moving. It's *swimming* there."

"What?" Gabriel couldn't wrap his mind around what a swimming Zero Fighter would mean.

She clicked again, and something bizarre happened between the shots: The cockpit of the plane had *bent* slightly, and was now *pointed* toward the container ship.

Next image: It was in the air. Somehow its metal wings had flapped down like a bird's, launching it into flight.

One more image, close and grainy: The seventy-five-year-old plane, seaweed and gunk dripping off it, was close to the camera. Its riveted sides had split, and through the seams Gabriel could make out shiny and mottled organic matter, like the skin of a squid. At the front of the plane, a long, jagged-toothed mouth had protruded, gaping wide and hungry. The Zero Fighter looked like it could *eat* the security camera.

And in the next image, it was nearly gone, its metal tail disappearing outside the frame along with the rest of its body.

"What *is* it?" Gabriel whispered.

"It's what everyone in the US Navy is worried about right now. Other than that I have no idea."

Gabriel thought. "It's a creature. Like some sort of… crustacean?"

"Well, everyone is calling them Lodgers."

"Them? There's more than one?"

"Yes. I saw one from the topside of the *Nebula*. That was an actual B-17. Come to find out they've been turning up for about three weeks."

"*Lodgers*," Gabriel repeated. "Because they lodge themselves inside discarded shells, like hermit crabs. Only instead of taking over the old shells of other creatures, they use old planes." He studied the vapor screen. "Back up a few images."

He pointed at the gaping mouth as Nerissa tabbed back. "Nasty teeth." Finally she displayed the third image, the first one where the creature looked like a mysterious plane bounding from the water. He almost couldn't find words. "I...So it takes up and wears a bomber, an actual man-made plane. That's *amazing*. I can't wait to show Misty and Peter this."

"Who?"

"Oh, I have a *crew* now. We do good work." He realized it had been a mistake to mention it the moment the words came out.

"Wait, *what*?" Nerissa's mouth hung open. "What do you mean, you have a crew?"

Gabriel winced. Half of him had hoped she would be impressed, but now he realized he should have known better. Even if it was almost exactly what she had done. "They're two crew members. I've trained them myself to man the *Obscure*."

"Gabriel, that's not the plan—who are these people?"

That really ticked him off. As if his sister had ever cared about his parents' plans. Their *plan* had been for both of their kids to live *the life obscure* like them, and then to gradually move into the world to see how they could bring… what did Dad call it? Their service? Nerissa had ditched the plan—and ditched Gabriel in the process. He didn't want to hear it about the *plan* from her.

"What?" he said. "I'm supposed to run the ship by myself?"

"First, *yes*, it can be run by one person."

"Not if things get complicated." Gabriel had an example right at hand, having just conducted a water rescue that had required Peter, Misty, and him with their hands full. "Running it by myself would mean basically cruising around, but if we're gonna do any sort of rescue…"

"Who are these people?"

"They're…classmates."

"Oh, for…" Nerissa closed her eyes. "No more. You're up on land to be an ambassador, not a recruiter. You're *different*, Gabriel. *Laws* up here are different. If you've been doing excursions with *students*? Stop it. I don't want to hear any more about this."

"I…"

"Okay?"

"Sure…sure, okay." He resolved that Nerissa would hear no more about this. Gabriel frowned and turned back to the image, ignoring his sister's distrust. She had a crew—why couldn't he? "Think about it, though. To wear a plane, it would have to either wrap itself around everything inside the plane or else it would have to scrape out the shell somehow. I have to see one of these. Are they all Zero Fighters or, wait . . . You mentioned a B-17 as well?"

Nerissa exhaled and responded, "Yes, but it goes beyond that. There's also a World War Two midget submarine, a couple more American B-17s, and something that witnesses say may be a sunken aircraft carrier."

"That would be . . ." Gabriel tried to remember how big an aircraft carrier was. While the Nemo family studied the navies of every nation, that didn't mean the details of every military branch stuck. ". . . enormous."

"About eight hundred feet long, and armored, with a mouth." Nerissa chuckled. "Thankfully that one doesn't seem to fly."

Gabriel's mind swirled with possibilities. "It doesn't make sense. I've never heard of these things before."

"Isn't that weird?" Nerissa asked. "Don't you think you would have by now, if they'd been out there? Don't you think *he* would have?" She meant their ancestor, the first Captain Nemo. Gabriel had digital copies of all of Captain Nemo's old journals, and while he hadn't read every one of them, he would have remembered machine-wearing creatures.

Gabriel nodded. "Giant creatures don't just appear out

of nowhere. Something would have to be happening to cause them to surface now."

"I'm with you on that. But that's not the real problem."

"What is?"

"The Lodgers attacked a US naval vessel. Last week. Damaged it severely. Now the navy is hunting them."

"*Hunting* them?"

"I've intercepted strict orders to the Pacific Fleet. They're to locate the Lodgers this week and, if they encounter a mass of them, prepare for an operation at noon Saturday. And they haven't gotten specific about this, but I think an *operation* could get out of hand quickly. In other words, about one week. They're not taking chances with something that could eat a nuclear submarine."

Gabriel gazed at the image. "You want me to save them." He pondered the long, nail-like teeth in the creature's mouth. That would be like her, to see this creature and instantly think to protect it from Man.

"Maybe?" Nerissa shrugged, suddenly looking more like the sister he'd known at Nemolab, who occasionally let slip that she didn't always know the next move. "You gotta see these things, Gabe. I want to know why they're here, and you know as well as I do that the Nemos can get that kind of information before the navy does."

"Okay, so . . . why aren't *you* doing this?" Gabriel asked, feeling a lump of excitement in his throat. A new species. Wow. "I mean, we could do it together."

She sighed. "Let's face it. I'm a target. Right before I saw the B-17, someone lured the *Nebula* with a decoy smuggler ship that turned out to be a trap. If I go running around getting in the navy's way with the *Nebula*—a sub that is on *everyone's* red list—I'll only make it more dangerous for the creatures. Right now, this is a Gabriel thing. Catch."

Nerissa tossed him a keychain-sized black object, and he caught it with one hand. It was a small, smooth stone about two inches long. A memory stick, basically, but only a Nemoship would be able to access it. "What's on here?"

"All the data I have on these creatures, including the coordinates where those shots were taken and where I had my encounter. Not much, I guess," she conceded.

Gabriel was thinking logistics. He could get away, but it would be better with his crew. "Seven days?"

She nodded and flipped off the light. Just then Gabriel began to hear the sound of a helicopter, a distant *whap-whap-whap* coming toward them. Over his shoulder he saw a heavy searchlight beam sweeping the surface of the water about three miles away.

Gabriel heard a *hiss* and *pop*, and the water nozzles on the projector buoy stopped spraying. The device's poles folded themselves down and disappeared into the ocean.

"I need to go before that chopper gets here. Look." Nerissa paused. Her face kept that infuriatingly serene veneer, but her eyes softened slightly. Sometimes tiny expressions were all you got with Nerissa. "I'm sorry it's like this."

"You're *sorry?* Sis. You can't keep blowing up ships. You have to stop."

"I'll stop when they stop." By *they* she meant a whole gallery of assailants of the sea, the whalers and the polluters and the pirates.

"They're never going to stop." *They're going to kill you*, he wanted to say. *I'm going to read in the news that they've finally—*

"That's probably the navy—go now." Nerissa revved the engine of her Katana. "I don't want you seen or arrested, certainly not because I dragged you out here."

Drag me? You didn't drag me, he thought. *If you asked me to meet you on the moon, I'd steal a rocket.*

"You don't have to worry about me." Gabriel revved his own Katana and steered away from the buoy. The chopper grew closer as its searchlight swept back and forth over the waves.

"I love you, little brother." The last word came as she disappeared into the sea.

Gabriel bit back the sting of her disappearance as he put his rebreather in his mouth. He dove just as the chopper arrived, its searchlight finding nothing but his wake.

6

ON MONDAY MORNING, Gabriel was at school an hour early, watching for Peter's and Misty's parents' cars. He checked his watch again at seven thirty, just as Ms. Kosydar's hatchback rolled into the little parking lot in front of the school. Good, good. They had half an hour to the first bell, and in that time the library would be open. They could talk there. No one ever went there.

When Peter swung open his door, Gabriel was bouncing his heels on the curb. "What?"

"You gotta see this." Gabriel slapped a stack of print-outs against Peter's chest. He put his hand on Peter's shoulder as they walked. "Library should be empty—" He turned back. "Hi, Ms. Kosydar!"

Ms. Kosydar nodded as she backed her car away. Just

then Misty came riding around the corner on her bike and Gabriel waved furiously, jogging to the bike rack. Peter jogged behind him with the printouts.

Misty eyed them both suspiciously as they ground to a halt in front of her. She clicked the lock on her bike. "What's with you?"

"Library—I have something to show you." Gabriel slammed through the double doors of the school and stayed ahead of them until they reached the big glass wall of the library.

He pushed open the library door, and Misty said, "I hate when you call me Library."

"Oh." He waggled his head sheepishly as he held the door. "Sorry. Good morning."

They headed back to a table at the far wall, nearly surrounded by books. Gabriel dropped his backpack on the table and looked at Peter, who still held the printouts. "You look at those yet?"

Peter smirked. "You *are* kidding, right?"

"Okay, put 'em down; let me show you this."

"You are *wired*, Gabriel," Misty observed. "I've never seen you like this. Did something go wrong with the rescue?"

"The what?" Gabriel was lost for a second as they sat down, and then he realized she was talking about the Friday-night adventure. That felt like *years* ago. "No, this is way bigger, *way* better than that."

"Whaaaat the heck are these?" Peter asked as he spread out the printouts of the Zero Fighter Lodger leaping over the cargo ship.

"Right." Gabriel slapped the table. "Exactly!"

Misty took one of the images, then set it down to "read" the other photos one after the other. "Go on."

"You're looking at an unknown race of creatures that has been turning up for the past several weeks. My sister gave me these images last night."

"You have a sister?" Peter asked. "Since when?"

"Since before I was born, but that's..." Gabriel waved his hand. "She's asked me to go find out about these things. And I have to hurry."

"Why do you have to hurry?" Misty asked.

"Because the navy is going to destroy them in less than a week."

"How many are there?"

"A lot more. But look. I'm here—my family is here—to answer the unknown questions." Gabriel hadn't really talked about his family much, but he wanted his friends to understand. He had a mission. "I need to find out what these things are and, if possible, stop them from being destroyed."

Peter leaned back. "Am I hearing this right?" He shrugged at Misty. "Is he telling us he's going to take on the navy?"

"It's not about taking anyone on. And anyway, I'm asking if *you* will."

Both of them were silent for a moment. Misty leaned forward. "Where were these photos taken?"

Gabriel pulled out a tablet and called up an atlas, then tapped in the coordinates as he spoke. "One hundred thirty-five degrees West…thirty-five degrees North." When he was done, he spun the tablet around so they could see the image of the ocean, with the coordinates highlighted.

"The Eastern Great Pacific Garbage Patch," Peter whispered.

Misty seemed to be searching her memory banks. "I've heard of that."

Peter spun his fingers in a swirl over the tablet. "There's a current called the North Pacific Gyre that swirls through the Pacific in a circle. And this, the Eastern Garbage Patch, is a giant whirlpool of plastic trash smack between Hawaii and California." A large oval representing the gyre glowed and revolved slowly in the middle of the ocean. "A lot of what we throw away breaks down and winds up there."

"Right." Misty remembered now. "It's a disaster for sea life, too. So how big is it?"

"About the size of Texas," Gabriel said. "Three hundred thousand square miles. Give or take."

"Yeah, so that's…big." Peter looked off. Gabriel could see him running calculations in his head, and then he looked back and laughed. "It would take the *Obscure* thirty hours just to get to the *edge* of that thing."

"Yeah," Gabriel answered. "And we've only got till

Saturday at noon. So if we leave tomorrow, we'll get out there sometime Wednesday and then have only a couple of days."

"Give or take," Misty repeated. "Plus if this event is on Saturday, then you're talking about getting back early Monday morning."

Gabriel nodded.

Peter took off his glasses and furiously polished them with his shirt. "Have you suffered some kind of brain damage from the breath-holding trick on Friday? Gabriel, it's October and we're in school."

"Well, we are *now*," Gabriel mumbled.

"Thousands of miles from home." Misty shook her head and pushed back from the table a little. "I mean, you can do anything, but we have parents."

"These things will *die*. And I need..."

Peter leaned in. "Hmm? What?"

Gabriel shrugged. His sister was completely wrong. He knew his ship, and he knew what it—what he—needed. "I need a crew."

"You're crazy. Forget it." Peter shook his head. Then he looked at Misty and laughed. "Nah, I'm just kiddin'. Of *course* I'm in."

"What? Really?"

"Absolutely." Misty laughed. "I was winking at Peter, like, two minutes ago. Nah. We'll do it."

Gabriel felt his face flush with relief.

"See, there's the blush. I love the blush." Peter pointed.

Misty snickered and then peered at Gabriel. "But how?"

Peter snorted. "I mean, we lie."

Misty rolled her eyes. "Get over yourself. You think you're such a great liar. What are we going to do, each say we're staying at someone else's house, and oh, by the way, we can't be reached? That'll work for twelve hours. Tops."

Gabriel got up, pacing. "A *week* gone. On a sea vessel. With limited ability to call home. That's not completely true—we could email."

"It's still a lot of time on a ship away from our parents," Misty pointed out. "I can't see how you just make something up. Even *us*."

Gabriel thought, looking across the library at the posters lining the glass wall. All kinds of club notices, bulletins. "What if it's *not* made-up?"

"What?" Peter asked.

Gabriel looked around at the library. "What if we... This is educational, right? We're in a STEM school, a science school. Peter, that volcano thing you did, how long was that?"

Peter thought for a second. "Six days. In Hawaii. But there were..."

"Who organized it?"

"I don't know, some foundation thing?"

"Right." Gabriel slapped the table again. "We don't lie. We make it real."

7

GABRIEL DIDN'T MAKE it to geometry, his first-period class. He sent a text and paced the upstairs bathroom for fifteen minutes with his backpack over his shoulder, dodging teachers and hiding in a bathroom stall when a pair of students came in. Then he snuck out. He took the back stairs, headed across the gymnasium, and exited through a door by a steep driveway blocked by concrete roadblocks that could be removed whenever the school decided to open that entrance up to delivery trucks.

He patted his bike where it rested on the bike rack next to the door, but left it there and headed up the sidewalk on foot. Less than thirty seconds later, a black Lincoln rolled by. The rear passenger door swung open, and he got in.

The car accelerated as Gabriel shut the door and

looked across the seat at a tall, thin man with scant hair over his ears and around the back of his head.

"Gabriel." The man smiled, but Gabriel could tell he wasn't sure why he was here.

"Hi, Mr. Zinoman."

Mr. Zinoman was the Nemos' lawyer. That was something else Gabriel had never needed to use before he'd surfaced. A man you could tell your secrets to. A man who *took care of things* for you. He had been chosen by Gabriel's parents, and Gabriel had learned to trust him. But he wasn't a parent, and part of Gabriel was kind of hurt that his own parents thought *go live on land by yourself and here's a guy who can sign stuff for you* was a winning plan.

"So ... I'm here," Zinoman moaned. He always seemed pained to talk to Gabriel, but Gabriel had learned it was just his way. He sounded busy. Gabriel wondered if Zinoman ever sounded anything but busy. "You asked me to be here, so I'm here."

Gabriel let his enthusiasm for the new mission take over. "I have some stuff I need to do. I took notes." Gabriel pulled his tablet out of his backpack and opened up a document into which he'd whispered the basics while he was waiting in the bathroom.

Zinoman looked at the tablet. "You're being squirrelly. Are you committing a crime?"

"What?"

"I just want to warn you that I can't be part of a crime."

"Come on," Gabriel scoffed. He cleared his throat as he looked over the list. "Here."

Zinoman took the tablet and read aloud, "'Oceanography and Stewardship Conference—Middle Grade Track.' I don't understand. You wouldn't get anything out of that; you're an oceanography expert. Is this something you want to support?"

"Oh, no, it's something I want to attend."

Zinoman shrugged and looked up. "Okay. Uh, sure. But wouldn't something like that be a little elementary for you?"

"Actually it's a little more complicated than just attending."

Zinoman grimaced. "I feel a headache coming on. Complicated how?"

"We need to create it."

"Create what?"

"The conference." Gabriel pointed at the tablet. "Keep reading."

"But—"

"Just read for a second."

Zinoman read the tablet again. "*Tomorrow?* That's—"

"Keep reading."

"'Peter Kosydar and Misty Jensen.' Who are they?"

Gabriel said, "They're two middle school students who I need to attend with me."

"'Sponsored by the Oceanographic Knowledge Consortium.' What's that?"

"That's a thing that somehow you've got to make happen in, like, twenty hours." Gabriel gestured at the tablet. "Take a look at the rest."

Zinoman read down for another minute and then looked up. "So let me see if I can summarize. You want to take yourself and your friends out of school for a week, and you want me to set it up so that you can say you're all going on a special field trip. On scholarship, I guess. All of it funded by your family."

"Yes."

Zinoman set down the tablet. "Gabriel...why?"

"Because." Gabriel understood. That reason wasn't in the notes. "My sister asked me."

"And if I send a message to Nemolab, what will your parents say?"

"You should do that." Gabriel nodded. "I haven't yet because I know them, and I know they wouldn't want me to come to them until I'd tried to work my way through it. But this isn't a secret from Mom and Dad. You should call them."

"I will."

"Okay." Gabriel meant it. "But we need to be out tomorrow. You'll need to have this figured out and call Harrison STEM by the end of school today. That's four o'clock. Peter and Misty and me need to get out and go straight to my house tomorrow, as soon as we can. So can you do it? Is it, like, impossible?"

"No, I can do it," the lawyer moaned. "This is...a challenge, but it's not impossible. I have a feeling you'll get to impossible eventually."

"Good." Gabriel looked out the window at the busy street. "Can you drop me off a block from where you picked me up? I need to sneak back in."

Zinoman relayed the request to the driver, and soon they were pulling up down the block from Harrison.

"Whatever you need. Call my parents." Gabriel got out and spoke as he held the door open. "If they object, then none of this happens. But if they trust me—and I think they will..." *Because it's for Nerissa*, he added silently. "I'll wait for your call."

Ocean Highway hummed with midmorning traffic as Gabriel walked along the sidewalk. How big was the biggest Lodger? How many of them were there? The photos his sister had shown him were tantalizing, but he ached to get underway.

"Gabriel!"

He looked up and saw Peter coming out the side door, glancing around before running out to walk back with him.

"What are you doing?" Peter asked.

"Seeing if we can make it official. I missed geometry."

"Not for the first time. Anyway, I wanted to catch you before you went back in." Peter pulled out his cell phone and swiped the screen on. "The Lodgers are in the news."

8

IT WAS TRUE. The Lodgers weren't being covered wall-to-wall on cable or anything—they were too weird to distract the country from its latest obsession, which was mainly about a war of insults on social media that Gabriel didn't bother to understand. But Peter had found references to strange creatures of metal in a handful of seafaring and navy-obsessed blogs. The theory seemed to be that people were seeing some kind of reflecting-light illusion. The US Navy had issued a predictable response to the science blog of one of the major papers: No comment.

All of that was good as far as Gabriel was concerned. The last thing he wanted was for the Lodgers to become *big* news, waking up the public and causing them to demand fast action from the government. People who lived on land didn't think about the sea very much in the day-to-day, and for once he was glad of it.

Gabriel walked his bike home, exchanging texts with Misty and Peter, telling them to wait and be ready. He felt the time gnawing at him as he waited for Zinoman to do his magic.

And then the moment of truth arrived.

They met in the library again the next day, and Gabriel did his best to hide his own worries about the plan. Misty and Peter arrived at the same time, both carrying duffel bags. That was a good sign.

"I'm sorry I wasn't able to text much." Misty dropped her duffel under the back table. She ran her fingers through her hair and secured it all with a navy-blue scrunchie. "My parents wanted a lot of answers, and it wasn't a good time."

Peter put his own duffel on the table and leaned back, balancing on the back legs of his chair as he polished his glasses. "What do you mean? What happened?"

"What kind of questions did they ask?" Gabriel gestured for her to go on. In fact Misty had texted him once, *Looks okay going to bed*, at about 9:30 P.M.

"Well, like, who was the sponsor, and I showed them the permission slip emailed to me from you, I mean your Mr....?"

Peter remembered. "Zinoman."

"And you didn't get any emails from me *and* him—just him," Gabriel reminded her. "I didn't send anything at all."

"Well, you were right. That guy's amazing. He even answered some emails they sent him."

Gabriel tapped the table. "Did they . . . seem suspicious?"

She shrugged. "After some basic answers from Mr. Zinoman, they were fine."

"Did he say he was going on the trip?"

She laughed. "He did *not*. I can't tell you how he maneuvered around that, but he was pretty slick. Wait, let's see." She pulled out her phone, opened an email, and read, "'They will be accompanied by and receive lectures from a selection of expert lecturers in marine biology and marine issues.'"

"Okay, *that's* the part I love." Peter looked at Gabriel. "A *selection*. I assume that selection of esteemed lecturers is *you*."

Gabriel laughed out loud. "You never know who else we might meet along the way."

"You really are a piece of work. But if it gets me out of school, it's solid in my book."

"Your mom didn't have a problem?" Gabriel asked.

"Nope." He shook his head in satisfaction. "I mean, I go on stuff all the time."

"That's the beauty of it," Misty agreed.

Gabriel looked at the time on his wristband. Five minutes to first period. He could have just stayed out and waited aboard the *Obscure*, but he'd wanted to make sure Misty and Peter could get away. And now the golden hour had come. "Okay. When the bell rings, we go to class. If everything went right with the school, then we'll be called out almost immediately."

"In other words, he had to do the same song and dance with the office that he did with our parents," Misty said.

Gabriel nodded.

Peter grew serious. "I gotta admit, that sounds tough."

"He has tricks." Gabriel had no idea what those tricks were, but there was a reason his parents trusted Zinoman to make things go smoothly.

Misty squinted. "Yeah, in your head you just said *I hope*, right?"

"Don't think about it. Peter, as soon as we're aboard . . ."

"Coordinates entered and we hightail it for the last known sighting spot." Peter nodded.

The bell rang and they all looked at one another. Gabriel breathed. "Okay."

Misty stood up. "Either we'll see you in a few minutes, or we won't."

Gabriel and Peter went to geometry and Misty went off to whatever she had—accelerated math, he thought.

Down the hall, amid the shouting of other students, Peter and Gabriel were silent. Either it would work or it wouldn't. Into class. They had a pair of desks in the back, and Peter dropped his duffel between them.

As the next bell rang and Mr. Terrill, the geometry teacher, stood up from his desk at the front, Peter leaned toward Gabriel. "Did we have homework?"

Gabriel laughed.

Mr. Terrill cleared his throat as he looked at a black leather notebook he had on the front desk. "Mr. Kosydar?"

Was this it?

"Sir?" Peter asked.

"If you look at question number one of the homework assignment…"

Peter went pale. Then a voice came on the intercom. "Would Peter Kosydar, Gabriel Nemo, and Misty Jensen please report to the front office?"

Mr. Terrill smirked. "Boy, are you lucky." He gestured for them to move on, and they hustled out.

Mr. Zinoman was waiting at the front office. And that was that.

~~~

Less than an hour later, the *Obscure* was underway.

On the bridge, Gabriel watched the screen as it displayed the rear cameras, water flowing with reflected glints of dust and tiny sea creatures over the glowing tail of the sub. He saw the metal structure where the *Obscure* rested at home shrink into the dimness as a tornadolike wake churned behind them. He switched to the foreground view, the vast ocean opening up before them.

Peter tapped away at his console. "Course is entered for the Great Pacific Garbage Patch. Time estimate just like I figured: thirty hours."

Misty whistled. "All the way to the middle of the ocean." She let it hang there. They had never gone that far out. "So what now?"

"I guess…" Gabriel closed the image and looked out at the sea. "Now we gotta figure out how to kill a day and a half."

9

GABRIEL LAY AWAKE on his bunk in the captain's quarters. He wasn't trying to sleep, although he should have been—instead, for now he was watching the water flow by outside the dark porthole to his left. A thought kept dogging him, and he didn't know how to put it away. Just how long did they *really* have? They were going out to investigate, to locate the creatures for themselves and learn what they could—but what if the creatures had destroyed a *passenger* ship by then? Would they be able to help at all? The truth was, there was no guarantee the navy would stick to its own Saturday deadline.

His room was curved, all wood and shining brass and mother-of-pearl, his clothes swaying in an open closet with the slight rock of the ship. A glint of light off the shoulder of one of his jackets caught his eye, and he smiled. Gabriel rose and went to the closet, pulling out a blue coat with gold piping at the collar and shoulders and the Nemo *N* at the throat clasp. This was a replica of the coat worn by his ancestor. It was too small for him now. It had been sewn by Mr. Chaudhari, the quartermaster at Nemobase, the island where the *Obscure* had been constructed. Gabriel had spent months living on the island, overseeing—well, consulting on at least—the construction of this sub. Mr. Chaudhari's father had been a tailor, and when the time to christen the ship had come, Mr. Chaudhari had presented Gabriel with the coat. Gabriel pulled back the collar and read the tiny script sewn inside: REMEMBER AND GROW.

Every Nemo had a motto, and this was his. He would apply it to everything. He would remember the past and learn from it. He would make the name of Nemo one of heroism and change.

Now that he thought about it, he had no idea what his sister's motto was.

A tablet on a small writing desk chirped, and sound waves beeped across the screen. "Captain?" Peter's voice. Peter was on watch until early morning, when Gabriel would take over for him. And next Misty, but since it was Gabriel's turn to sleep, she was free to either sleep or entertain herself somehow or another.

Gabriel tapped the screen. "What's up?"

"Just wondering if you were awake."

"Well, I am now, either way."

"Good. You want to see some whales?"

On the bridge, Misty had already arrived, and she and Peter were standing at the front screen. The moment Gabriel entered he froze, momentarily caught up in sheer awe.

A shape nearly the size of the *Obscure* came into view from above, its tapered nose flowing past the front camera and on, and on, and on. To the right and left, a tail appeared, slowly whipping the water. The whole of the ship bobbed slightly.

"Oscillators?" Gabriel felt the floorboards vibrate a little faster.

"Working overtime to keep us steady."

"Good. We don't want to upset them."

They were in the middle of a pod of gray whales. The ship was doing forty knots, almost forty-six miles an hour, and great blue-gray forms swam over, under, and around them.

"Look at that." Misty steepled her fingers in front of her mouth as the smooth tail of the one traveling over them came into view and whipped around. "It's as big as we are."

"Almost." Gabriel couldn't help smiling. He looked at a sonar reading in the corner of the main screen and saw a mass of them over the green dot that represented the *Obscure*.

"This is the great spring migration!" Misty looked at

him with a matching smile. "I've only *read* about it. They'll travel all the way past Washington State, two thousand miles from Mexico."

"Turn on the mics," said Gabriel excitedly. "Let's hear them."

"Aye." Peter hit a switch on the wall. "Here we go."

At first there was static, and then the external mics came online and they heard it: what sounded like a forest of drums, beating steadily, *boom-boom-boom*, rising up and falling down, hundreds of higher and lower drumbeats sounding away as the whales passed around them. Around that sound were other percussive sounds: watery pops and gurgles, rhythmic and slow and mixed amid the drumbeats.

"I thought whales *sang*." Peter wrinkled his brow.

Misty nodded. "Some do. Gray whales communicate with this drumming sound."

"What does it mean?"

"No one knows. We don't even know how they do it."

Gabriel closed his eyes, listening to the burbling noises, the drums, and the brush of the water against the microphones. *We live on a world of mostly water,* he thought, *and we don't understand its kings at all.*

He looked at Misty. "You know what these whales used to be called? Devil Fish. Because when they were attacked by whalers, they put up a fight. *We* attacked *them*, and we blamed the whales for the violence that followed. We've nearly erased them from existence, and we don't even know why they sound like drums. We do it again and again. We're doing it now." Gabriel opened his eyes and looked back. "We have a responsibility. To figure out what to do before the same thing happens to the Lodgers."

10

LATE WEDNESDAY AFTERNOON, Peter was on watch again while Misty slept in her bunk off the dive room and Gabriel exercised in the passenger room. Peter called with the news. "Gabe? We're reaching the Garbage Patch."

"Really?" Gabriel reached the bridge a minute or two ahead of Misty, who rubbed her face and shook off whatever sleep she'd had as she reached her console. The *Obscure* was running along the surface as Gabriel gazed at the view screen, which still showed endless Pacific blue ahead.

"Yep." Peter threw the sonar up, and it took over half the screen. As the sonar line swept around in clocklike circles, countless speckles flickered dully. "It *covers* the ocean up ahead. And it'll keep going."

"But I can't see anything at all." Misty watched the waves on camera.

"I think the plastic beads float just under the water, basically," Peter said.

A new ping appeared at the top edge of the sonar screen—a thick mass that indicated something with a lot of weight. "Hello," Gabriel said. "What's that?"

Peter touched his headphones. "It's not making any noise. If it's a craft, it's not running. In fact it's not moving."

"Could it be a fishing vessel?" Gabriel asked. "Maybe they're anchored."

"If so, I'd be hearing all kinds of things. Tools, machinery, generators."

"Besides," added Misty, "would a fishing boat be all the way out here?"

Gabriel shrugged. "Could it be a whale?"

"Like a *dead* whale?" Misty asked. "Maybe a small one."

"About thirty feet long, yeah," Peter agreed. "Do dead whales float?"

It was Misty's turn to shrug.

"Okay, how far is that?" Gabriel asked. It was still not visible onscreen, but they were moving toward it at twenty-six knots.

"Just over the horizon," Peter said. "About twenty-five miles."

Gabriel scratched his head. "Prepare to dive to sixty-five feet."

"What do you want to do?" Misty asked. "Are we going around it?"

"Nah. I want to get a closer look."

Peter said, "Dive sixty-five feet, aye." Water started pounding inside the walls as they dropped below the surface, and the front cameras filled with what looked like snow in the froth of the waves. In fact the snow was garbage, millions of clumps of white, gray, blue, and green beads battering softly against the front of the ship.

"There's your garbage." Peter nodded toward the screen.

"Pellets," Gabriel observed.

"It's amazing." Misty sounded angry. "You take a soda bottle and grind it for years, and it turns to a bunch of BBs."

"It's disgusting." Gabriel had seen too many images of fish cut open, their bodies filled with plastic waste. "People are killing the ocean and they don't even know it."

The sound of the pellets created a constant patter on the hull, and Gabriel had to raise his voice slightly. "How far down does this stuff go?"

"Reaching sixty-five feet," Peter reported. "And we're still in it."

"Ugh. Steady as she goes."

As they moved along below the waves, Peter called out the distance to the strange whale or boat or whatever it was. Gabriel watched the sonar screen as the shape got closer to the center. It still lay motionless on the surface.

"Come to about a hundred yards from its position and full stop."

"Aye." A few minutes later, Peter announced that they were there. "Full stop."

"Periscope depth."

"We're gonna use the periscope?" Misty asked. "I love that."

Gabriel felt the ship rising as water rushed out of the walls and tanks, and something caught his ear. "What's that noise?"

Peter frowned. "If I had to guess, I think there's a lot of sludge in the water moving in and out of the ballast tanks. Garbage. It's making the water pump out a little slower."

"Huh. Efficiency?"

"Ninety-four percent. Just slows the tanks down a little."

"Wait," Misty said with concern. "That doesn't sound good. How do you know it won't get worse?"

"Ninety-four percent is pretty good," Gabriel insisted, but in the back of his head he didn't feel so sure. "Don't worry. I built this thing." *But that isn't saying as much as you'd like, is it? You don't know everything that can happen to these engines.*

Misty looked at him for a second and nodded.

"Periscope depth, Captain," Peter reported.

"Deploy periscope."

"Deploy periscope, aye."

"Onscreen."

They heard a ratcheting as a metallic cable shot from the body of the *Obscure* and the view screen filled with a camera image—the camera was shooting through teeming masses of plastic muck for a moment, and then the sun broke through and the camera splashed out onto the surface. The periscope camera was atop a Frisbeelike disc that rested on the water. They were still staring up at the sky when the end of the cable straightened above the disc, popping the camera down into position. Now they were looking out across the ocean.

Misty's tone brightened as she watched the new image. "See, I like this because you get to see the ocean as though you're not there at all, just a floating *you* and all that blue."

"Beats the heck out of a pipe with mirrors," Peter agreed. That was the way old periscopes worked.

"Don't knock a pipe with mirrors; we have that too in case this thing doesn't work," Gabriel said. "Show us the object."

Peter turned a tiny joystick on the right of his console, and the camera slowly swept across the horizon clockwise, then stopped.

Floating on the surface was a boat with blue walls and a small white pilot house, which was where the captain would stand and steer the vessel and, if needed, radio for help. *Yep.* Gabriel sighed. "It's a fishing trawler."

Peter clicked his tongue. "Anybody else disappointed it's not an unknown creature?"

"Not me." Misty looked relieved. "I'm just glad it's not a dead whale."

"Can you make out markings?" Gabriel asked.

Peter magnified the image until they could see the boat, floating loose. They saw a series of markings on the side and AGIMARK INDUSTRIES written in white letters.

Misty turned to her station and tapped the name into a search engine. "Well, that's a fishing company. Of course." She looked back. "I don't find anything on this particular boat. What do you want to do?"

"So…you come across a dead ship." Gabriel rubbed his hands, thinking through the problem. "What if they had engine trouble? If they were blown off course, there could be people on it. Except…"

He was thinking about the story his sister had told him about the fake whaling vessel.

"Except what?" Misty asked. "Are you afraid of what we might find?"

"Ugh. I'm not afraid," he said. "I'm just wondering, what if it's a decoy?"

She raised her eyebrows as if he were insane.

"Look, my sister said that someone deliberately drew her to a boat that turned out to be a trap."

"Okay." Misty smirked. "So your many enemies are so

good, they know just where you're going to be coming, down to fifty or so miles? In thousands of miles of ocean?"

He had to admit that Misty was right. Nerissa's paranoia was contagious. He had to watch to not pick it up. "Nah, you're right. And anyway, if there could be people who need help..."

"Then we do what we do."

But he *was* afraid of something else that was a lot more likely. Gabriel didn't want to think about how the odds were that those stranded people had been out here too long and it was already too late. And besides that, they were silent. He had a sick feeling that they were about to see something awful.

He nodded. "Peter, bring the dinghy online."

"Aye." He brought up a diagram of the *Obscure* onscreen, and Gabriel saw a compartment on the starboard-side rear, near the dive room, light up.

"Away we go." He turned and gestured to Misty as he headed to the door of the bridge.

At the back of the bridge before they entered the corridor, Gabriel put his thumb to a biometric scanner and unlocked a locker next to the door. He drew out a pair of long green composite-plastic rifles. Because of the red, clawlike stinger on the end, they called them pincer guns.

He handed one to Misty and took the other.

"You sure we need these?" She pulled back a cocking

slide, and a pair of pincers at the end of her rifle began to crackle with energy. She kept the barrel pointed at the deck. It wasn't supposed to be lethal—none of Gabriel's weapons were—but they were both sticklers about keeping anything remotely dangerous pointed away from people, including yourself, unless you meant it.

"Only if it's a trap."

Gabriel held up his rifle with his finger at the selector switch, a small knob next to the trigger that looked like the horn of a narwhal, the unicorn of the sea. "Keep it set for local. That way it's like . . ."

Misty held hers out. "Like a Taser." She nodded and cocked the pincer.

They moved quickly down the corridor, through the passenger compartment to the end where a porthole blinked with red lights from top to bottom. Gabriel touched the scanner and the door flew open.

The Nemotech escape dinghy, a small craft that Gabriel rarely used, was about the size of a small fishing boat, with two forward chairs and bench seats of metal in the back. It had huge forward windows but, of course, all they could see as they strapped in was a bare metal wall. Gabriel and Misty put in earpieces as Gabriel reached up and toggled a switch labeled HOUSING.

The wall in front of them, part of the side hull of the *Obscure*, slid back, and the dinghy was enveloped in water and garbage pellets. He could barely see out the window for the swirling of tiny bits of plastic. He yanked down a handle in the roof labeled DEPLOY. "Here we go."

Clamps on the side of the dinghy drew back, and they dropped like a stone into the ocean below. "Engines?"

Misty hit a button. "Engines, aye," and the small rear engines cut on, shuddering and causing the whole craft to vibrate. Gabriel grabbed a joystick in front of him and drew back, and they sailed below the *Obscure*. Through the garbage beads he saw the nose of the *Obscure* come into view and disappear as they shot into the water beyond, and then he pushed the stick forward and they rose.

They bobbed up onto the surface, and bits of plastic clung to the windows. He hit another switch and the sunshields drew back, leaving the entire top half of the dinghy clear. It was like floating in a Nemoglass bubble.

"Good *grief*, it's bright." Misty squinted and spread her palm over her face.

"Yeah, sorry. I just wanted to be able to see all around."

The afternoon sun beat down mercilessly, creating blinding flashes off the ocean. The ship bobbed slightly on temperate waves. He couldn't have asked for a calmer sea.

Gabriel drew them closer to the fishing vessel, which still looked dead.

"Watch out for trawling nets." Misty pointed at the cranelike apparatus on the back of the boat, from which long fishing nets dangled loose into the water. He nodded and piloted the dinghy around to the fore of the fishing vessel.

"There's a ladder." Gabriel drew them close to a metal structure that ran down the side of the boat. He deployed a grabber cable from the side of the dinghy, and it latched on to the ladder. "Okay?"

"Looks good to me."

"Peter," Gabriel called. Peter was still on the bridge. "We're boarding."

They unstrapped, grabbed their pincers, and went to the back of the dinghy, where Misty twisted a pair of handles on the starboard side. She swung the dinghy's door open and stood on the threshold. She stepped from the dinghy, put her foot on the ladder, and started to climb, and he followed her.

Gabriel waited to grab the ladder until Misty had poked her head over the top of the bulwark, the little wall that ran around the deck of the ship. Misty looked around, then back down to Gabriel. "Nothing yet." She climbed over the top of the ladder and he heard her drop to the deck on the other side, and in a moment he had landed there as well.

The gray metal deck was filmed over with beads of plastic that squished under their feet as they stepped through. Obviously the boat had been here long enough to be hit by a few really big waves that had sent beads of plastic sloshing across the deck. Speaking of big waves, the bulwark around the deck only came up to Gabriel's hips, so he could easily see someone being swept over if they weren't being careful.

Here and there ropes and equipment fastened to poles along the inside of the bulwark swayed gently with the boat. The pilot house stood at the back, next to a small unused escape dinghy still tied to the deck.

"Getting that little boat into the water is easy." Misty pointed to a series of ropes and pulleys attached to the escape dinghy. "You just lift it and drop it over the side. So why is it still here?"

"I don't know," he said. "But it's not a good sign. This whole boat looks empty. *Hellooo?*" he shouted.

The fishing boat was as silent as a tomb. If anyone *was* here, they must be too sick or exhausted to move. He and Misty would have to look for them. The two exchanged glances, caught up in the eerie quiet.

"Hellooo?" Misty called as she stepped farther across the deck. "Hull first, or the pilot house?"

"I think it's empty," Gabriel said. And at this point he was hoping so. He spoke into the microphone at his throat. "Peter, we're looking around." He gestured across the deck and shrugged at Misty. "Let's check out the pilot house."

They squished through the beads of plastic until they reached the pilot house, its windows bare except for sludgy streaks of plastic beads where waves had whipped up and struck them.

The door was open, and Gabriel went in first. The emergency telephone was off its hook, the handset dangling against the floor. A metal cover for a notebook sat next to the steering column, and he went to open it as Misty came in behind him.

He unlatched the metal and found a paper notebook inside. "It's the captain's log."

"What does it say?"

Gabriel flipped the pages and scanned the writing before him.

- Ø3ØØ 13 MARCH, ENGINE TROUBLE...

- 15ØØ 13 MARCH, HEART ATTACK AND SOS

- 23ØØ 15 MARCH...

"They were rescued. These guys had engine trouble and a medical emergency. Looks like they got rescued by someone else from the fishing company."

Peter's voice came back through Gabriel's earpiece. "Okay."

"So that's that," Gabriel said, relieved.

Misty visibly relaxed. "Okay. But why leave the boat?"

"They were in a hurry—maybe they planned to come back and just haven't yet. Anyway, there's nothing for us to do." Gabriel looked at the beads of plastic. "I really don't like being here."

"I'm glad *you* said it."

"Captain?" Peter's voice had an urgent sound.

"Yes?"

"Something just appeared on the scope!" Peter said quickly. "I don't know what it is, but it's *big*. I think it came from deep down."

"What do you mean, *big*?"

"Big like a whale," Peter said. "But the shape is wrong."

Gabriel spun around, scanning the water, but what good was that when he couldn't see under the *boat* they were standing on? "Where is it now?"

"It's coming your—"

And then the boat rocked hard, and Gabriel and Misty went flying.

11

GABRIEL'S SHOULDER SANG with pain as he slammed into a pole. He grunted and rolled over, standing up. Misty had collided with a coil of ropes and got up just as quickly, no worse for the wear. They ran to the bulwark around the deck, looking out.

"What hit us?" Misty asked.

"What do you see, Peter?" Gabriel scanned across the water, but all he saw were undisturbed waves. He rubbed his sore shoulder. He was lucky he hadn't broken a collarbone. Boy, that would be great, to be all the way out here with no doctor. He didn't even want to think about the pain, or the fact that they'd have to turn back. He could have lost the whole assignment from his sister just by being clumsy. He should know how to roll better. *Misty* knew how to roll.

Misty crossed the deck as Peter said in Gabriel's earpiece, "I see one—no, two—shapes in the water. One is moving away..."

"There!" Misty shouted, and Gabriel ran to her side. He saw a missilelike shape moving fast just below the surface, away from the boat.

"The first shape is right under the stern," Peter hissed.

The boat rocked hard toward the rear as water splashed. A strange call warbled across the air.

Misty shouted toward the stern of the boat. "It's there..." And that was all she got out before she stopped, her mouth hanging open in a perfect O.

All the world slowed to a crawl as Gabriel felt adrenaline wash through his system, his chest tightening.

A great tentacle the size of a fire hose flew up over the rear of the craft and slapped down. Metal popped and groaned. Gabriel and Misty struggled to keep their feet.

Misty backed up, spitting out her words. "We gotta get off this boat." A hissing sound came from where the tentacle landed, and Gabriel smelled burning paint. The end had a wide, flat, leaflike sort of frond, and as the frond vibrated, metal began to melt. The tentacle punched through the deck as another one came roaring up from below, whipping from the side, landing near Gabriel's feet.

He stared at it. Small shapes he could only describe as *bulbs* vibrated on the frond, folding back their husks and emitting a red, burning core. The tentacle swept toward him, and he hopped away.

"The second creature is coming back toward you on the starboard side!" Peter shouted in his earpiece.

Gabriel heard a loud splash and looked out to the water. The missile shape was coming fast.

Just then, the owner of the two tentacles they'd seen so far started climbing up and poked its head into view.

Gabriel gasped despite himself.

What in the name of all the oceans is that?

It had a long snout like the head of a crawfish, with multiple tentacles moving around, feeling along the deck. It was calling loudly.

"Look out!" Misty cried as another tentacle flew up and swept toward her on the deck. She backed up against the starboard bulwark, cut off.

Gabriel triggered his pincer gun and jammed it into the tentacle, and the creature screamed, jerking the tentacle away. The crazy tentacle frond jiggled in the air above their heads as Misty joined Gabriel at the center of the craft.

There was another roar in response, and Gabriel looked back out to the water.

Something was rising from the waves. Gabriel saw the propeller first, looking like a nose as eyes protruded above. Four wings emerged next, two stacked on each side. The creature whipped its wings and rose, plastic beads and water streaming down as it took to the air. It was a World War I biplane. For a moment Gabriel was stunned, taking in the strange tentacles hanging from the body of the plane and the faded blue barnacled tail, split into sections and pulsating with strange flesh and tendrils swishing from side to side as it swooped toward them.

The biplane was approaching swiftly, angrily, flapping its wings in a way biplanes were never meant to do.

No, no, no, this was too much. What was he thinking? This wasn't a *slide show*; he was about to get himself and his friend eaten by an airplane.

Shut up! he shouted at his own thoughts. *Move.* "We're done. Get to the ladder." They staggered with the rocking of the boat as the bigger creature steadily tried to eat—*put on?* he thought wildly—the fishing boat from the tail up.

He had seen the images Nerissa had gathered and thought he was prepared to see one of the Lodgers, but now that he was faced with *two* of them, he realized he had been a complete fool. He wasn't prepared for the *alienness* of them, the bizarre transfiguration that went into taking human machines—machines of war—and wearing them. In the library he'd approached them like a scientist, but in person he was near frozen with fear.

No. Don't give in to fear. Fear is not your enemy. It's just there. The adrenaline pulsing through you isn't the enemy. It's just getting your body ready. What's the enemy? Freezing. That's the enemy. You're afraid? Just don't freeze.

The biplane twisted in the air, bending its body like an Olympic diver headed for the pool. It hit the water and disappeared under the starboard side, crashing along the hull as it went.

The shock sent them stumbling into each other, pellets flying under their feet as they scrambled toward the ladder on the port side. Misty reached it first, holding back her hand to grab Gabriel and help him up. She put her hands on the railing of the ladder, preparing to climb over.

That was when the biplane rose again at the side of the boat, not far from the ladder and the dinghy, their only way off. He could see its face now, bulbous, with great snail-like stalk eyes which swiveled as it sat, its wings undulating as its eyes finally found Gabriel and Misty.

"*Yahhhh!*" was the only word Gabriel could think of as they shrank back. The creature opened its mouth underneath the propeller, showing rows and rows of thin whales' teeth. The whole metal body pulsed up and down slightly under the water, and Gabriel backed up. It looked ready to pounce.

The creature whipped its body hard and smashed into the dinghy with its tail, tearing the boat free and sending it bobbing away.

No! That's our way off.

Okay. Okay. "Peter!" Gabriel called as he and Misty

moved back, trying not to slip, toward the center of the boat. "We've lost the dinghy; we need you."

Peter didn't hesitate. "I'm coming to get you."

Misty shouted, "How close can you get? They're focused on the aft and port side now. I guess we'll head as far forward and starboard as we can?" She made eye contact with Gabriel, and he nodded quickly.

A roar came from the rear as the giant crawfish continued climbing upward, bulwarks snapping as tentacles swarmed the deck.

Gabriel wanted to scream.

Gabriel and Misty reached the starboard side at the bow of the boat and looked out. All they could see were beads of plastic floating in the water. Those things could choke you in an instant, he realized. "Try not to breathe in any of that gunk when we get in the water. Peter, where are you?"

"Right here," came Peter's voice, as the platform of the *Obscure* broke the surface two hundred yards away to their right.

A tentacle swept toward Gabriel from the rear of the boat, and he turned his pincer on it, sending a sizzling arc of electricity. The arc impacted the thing's flesh, and smoke rose off it. The creature screamed again.

In response, the biplane leapt out of the water, landing on the starboard side of the deck, and started scuttling toward them, lashing out with its tentacles. Misty cried out as one of the tentacles smashed against her shoulder and her pincer went clattering. It wrapped around her waist, lifting her, and Gabriel yelled. He fired again, sending an arc of energy over Misty's shoulder into the tentacle. The biplane screamed and dropped away from the boat.

Misty dropped to her knees, shaking. "Shockkk..."

"I know, I know, I'm sorry, come on." Gabriel slung his pincer onto his shoulder and pulled her to her feet. Shakily, they began to climb over the side. "*Keep fighting*, come on."

Misty was still stunned; the shock of the pincer arc had sizzled through her and left her barely awake. *Idiot*, he told himself. *Idiot. You've made this a disaster.* "Here we go."

The shock of the water hit him as he came up under Misty, his arm around her and his hand under her chin. He began to kick, swimming backward toward the *Obscure*. Two hundred yards to safety. There were beads every-where. Gabriel even felt some of them on his lips as he spat them away and shouted to Peter: "Move sideways toward us and spring the hatch!"

A hatch popped open on the platform as Gabriel and Misty neared the side of the *Obscure*. "Come on!" Peter shouted in his ear.

Waves were lapping over Gabriel and Misty, and he prayed the biplane was done for now. "Misty, wake up," Gabriel hissed. "Wake up, I need you."

Just kick. Just keep kicking.

His back slammed into the bulkhead of the *Obscure*, and he turned, pulling Misty toward a ladder a little way ahead on the ship. Realizing there was no way he could lift her up and climb at the same time, Gabriel fumbled, trying to loop her arm through the ladder.

Misty sucked in air and jolted in his arms. "I'm awake, I'm awake."

But she wasn't. *Not awake enough, Gabriel, can't you see that? And you can't very well lift her up a ladder yourself, can you?*

He shook his head. *Come on, solve it, solve it.*

There was a hook, a lassolike rescue hook fastened to the railing of the platform. He could use that. *Yes. Now you're thinking.*

"Here, here. Hold on." Gabriel put Misty's hand on the ladder and felt her grip it before he let go, scrambling up. At the top, he unfastened the hook. It was a loop of cording at the end of a two-foot-long pole. He held the pole, pointing the lasso end toward the water. He thumbed a small trigger on the side of the pole, and it clattered out another eight feet, the lasso splashing into the water next to Misty. *At least that worked. But now you have to use it.*

It took two tries, even with Misty's help as she came to more and more, to get it under her shoulder.

Misty shook her head as she climbed up the ladder, the rescue hook pulling her as she went. She shook her whole body as if wringing it out and scowled. "Did you *shock* me?"

"I know!" he said again as she climbed down into the hatch. "It was an accident, I'm sorry!"

Gabriel waited till she had gone through the hatch before he dared to look back at the fishing trawler. The boat was smoking and swarming with tentacles now. He saw the trawler's seams rip apart and tentacles burst forth up and down its side.

The biplane had left the trawler's deck already and was sticking up out of the water, its bulb eyes swiveling toward Gabriel and the *Obscure*. Locking onto them, he realized.

Gabriel pulled the hatch closed.

12

"PETER, GET US out of here!" Gabriel shouted as he came down the ladder into the bridge.

"You don't have to ask me twice." Peter shoved the throttle stick forward. "Man, are you guys all right?"

"What *was* that?" Misty demanded. Absently she ran her fingers through her hair, and a few burned pieces fell out. "Ugh. You singed me. Saved me but *singed* me."

"I know!" Gabriel slumped, wringing his hands. "I know, and I'm sorry. I didn't think that would happen." *Because you've never fired those things under any kind of pressure before, have you?*

"I know, I know," Misty said. "It's just hair, it...grows back."

"Were those *them*?" Peter demanded. "Were those the *Lodgers*?"

"I think so." Gabriel quickly went to stand at the front, leaning on the stations below the view screen.

"Are you telling me we came out here to study those things and they tried to eat you?" Peter shouted.

"One of them was trying to put on the trawler, I think. The other one seemed to be acting as a guard," Gabriel said.

"Why did it attack us?" Misty asked. She sounded hurt, and with good reason. But it was more than physical. Up to now they had been thinking of this as some sort of mercy mission, but the creatures they were here to help hadn't seen them as anything but a threat. He knew he had no right to, but he felt genuinely betrayed.

Don't be ridiculous. Would you feel betrayed by a shark?

"I think it was just bad luck," Gabriel said finally. "I don't know; I think they attacked us because we were threatening. And then when I used the pincer on a tentacle to get one of the Lodgers out of the way, the other one flipped out."

"People aren't gonna be too patient if they keep trying to kill anyone who gets in their way," Peter grumbled as he steered the ship.

"*Argh*. We're supposed to be studying these things, not antagonizing them."

"Who's antagonizing who?" Misty harrumphed.

The whole ship rocked with a new collision.

"What was that?" Gabriel glanced around the walls of the bridge. "I'm bringing up the side cameras." He went to a console on the wall and quickly brought up a menu that usually showed on Misty's station. He didn't want to ask her. *Sorry you were nearly electrocuted; can you get right on bringing up pictures for us?*

When he switched to the side cameras, the radar map that filled the main screen dissolved into an underwater image lit by floodlights, plastic blobs making the image snowy. Nothing. He panned down.

The ship shook again, two solid *whumps* in rapid succession.

The camera's view moved downward until he could see the side of the *Obscure*. The biplane had grabbed onto the submarine and was chewing on the side, its lower wings flapping against the ship as its upper wings floated free in the water.

The biplane pulled free a strip of mother-of-pearl, shaking its snout, letting the strip of rocklike substance fall free.

That was not good. There were a lot of layers to the *Obscure*'s hull, but every piece yanked away was one piece closer to the real enemy: *water.* Whatever a submarine might face—enemy weapons, enemy subs, mines—all of those were just tools that other people used to let the water in. To let it crush you by ripping the body of your ship open.

They were under attack now, and if he didn't figure out the right thing to do to help his friends and hope they could figure out the right things, too, it would end just one way: death.

Gabriel thought about all of this and could feel his skin tingling, because if something tore the *Obscure* apart, it would tear his friends apart as well.

He touched his shaking right hand with his left. But he could not let his crew see just how scared he felt. Not because it would embarrass him, although it would. Not because it would frighten them, although that was certain. But because if he showed that fear now, if he let his voice quiver now, it would throw them off, and they would make mistakes, and then *he* would make mistakes. And that was how people died.

Another crash, this one sending shivers through the *Obscure* from the front.

"Oh, boy, Peter," he said. "Let's move."

"Cameras are my thing, Gabriel," Misty said, and he turned to look at her. "Let me take that." She was hunched over her station with her hands on the menus. She *seemed* to have recovered.

Or was he just telling himself that? "Are you sure you're a hundred percent?"

She shook her head and smiled a little insincerely. "Hundred percent, but we are *definitely* going to talk about this."

Okay, so he was in trouble. "Absolutely. Front cameras."

Misty brought up the cameras showing the prow of the ship. They had picked up another Lodger—an old, small submarine, probably Russian, was curling around the prow of the *Obscure* and chewing on it. It blocked the camera as the rusted metal and undulating tendrils swished back and forth. Sharp teeth gnashed in close view.

Knock it loose. It's gonna tear us open. "Peter, dive ten meters."

"Dive, aye."

The *Obscure*'s prow dipped as they picked up speed and the submarine creature lost its grip, dropping out of sight for a moment.

"Rear camera?" Gabriel hoped there weren't any more around. Through the snowy image he could see the bi-plane, still in pursuit. Then the submarine they had knocked off the prow soared into view from the side.

It grew in size now, and Gabriel realized with a sinking sensation that the creatures were drawing closer.

"They're gaining on us," Peter said.

"Copy that."

Misty spoke clearly and slowly. "Gabriel, what do you want to do?"

"Ideas?"

"We could keep running," Misty said. "They're biological; they might tire out."

Peter scoffed. "Or what, we lead them to Japan? They'll love that. The Japanese, I mean."

"Are you recommending we shoot at them?" Gabriel asked. "On our first encounter, we fire pincer missiles at them?"

"They're just energy missiles," Misty said. "It should just stun them. I think."

"Yeah, exactly," Gabriel said.

Misty shook her head. "We need to see all around. I'm bringing up the front and back cameras." The screen split. On the left side of the screen, they saw the nose of the *Obscure* as water swished over the top, garbage-filled blackness as far as they could see.

On the right, the pursuing creatures split up, the submarine aiming for their hull and coming fast.

It was aiming its hard nose at them, coming at them like a torpedo.

"Evasive maneuvers," Gabriel said. "Grab onto something."

Peter yanked the stick, and they swung hard to the left and dipped, putting distance between themselves and the submarine creature. But the movement slowed them down, and now both the creatures closed in again.

Peter shoved the throttle forward and the engines rumbled harder.

On the right screen, the little biplane fluttered slightly,

changing its position and moving off in the water. The submarine fell back and rose to the side as well.

"Uh-oh," Misty said. "I think they're getting out of the way of something."

At first all he could see was a large swirl of displaced plastic beads. Then, bursting from the darkness below, a massive shape swam up and pulled into view.

Gabriel's first thought was *whale*—not a real whale, but a big, fat, wide cartoon whale that swallowed fishermen and boys, an angry, hungry thing of myth. It was vast, some forty feet across and surely longer, though he couldn't see the whole thing. Its skin was a pulsing, tentacle-teaming fabric of rusted metal strips and iron panels covered in a crazy patchwork of rotting wooden planks black with moss and aged grime. Its eyes peered out from crooked holes on either side of the ancient prow. Broken masts and tarry British banners flapped and flopped across its deck. Its nose was a long, crooked beam of waterlogged oak slicing toward them. And below this it had a mouth—no, *two* mouths, one the ripped and jagged armor of metal and rotted wood, and the other, behind that, a hungry maw of needle teeth.

"What in heck is *that?*" Peter asked.

"I . . ." Gabriel couldn't believe the next words to come out of his mouth. "That . . . is a British man-of-war."

The creature took the lead and barreled toward them, looking to batter them with its iron-plated nose.

"And it's fast…okay, belay, forget maneuvering. Dive."

"*Dive*, aye," Peter echoed. The nose of the *Obscure* dipped, and Gabriel rocked on his heels as they slid downward in the water, picking up speed as they went. But now he heard a mechanical groaning inside the *Obscure*.

"What's that?"

Peter scowled. "Engines are fighting the plastic sludge in the water, Gabe. Depth four hundred feet and diving."

The man-of-war creature altered its course to match them.

Misty pointed a thumb at the screen. "Can that thing catch us?"

"It won't." Gabriel hoped that was true.

But it was moving faster now, the great body zooming toward them. *Of course the Lodgers would have remarkable moving power*, he thought. They had to be incredibly strong to soar out of the water the way they did. He doubted very much that anything as big as a British man-of-war could lift itself out of the water, but they were in *its* element now.

A huge burst of bubbles, some unknown gas, spewed from the man-of-war, and it picked up speed.

"Oh, my…" Gabriel stared, his mind flip-flopping madly between fear of being crushed in the jaws of a living ship and pure amazement at the wonder of the thing. Had his sister felt the same way when she saw them first? "They have some way of pushing out air to get heavier. A natural *ballast* system."

"Yeah, that's *fascinating*," Peter said. "It's gaining on us. We are at six hundred feet and diving, and that thing is definitely closing."

A high-pitched beep erupted from Misty's station and started repeating. "Proximity alert, Captain." The beeping continued.

"Uh…okay. Forget diving. Expand gases and surface again. Maybe the sudden change of direction will—"

"Aye." A distant hissing came from the bulkheads as chemical reactions fired and oxygen flowed into the ballast tanks. They pitched upward, heading for the surface once more. "Crap, we're getting sixty percent of the power we should. And we're hot; the engines are running hot."

"Come on; give up," Gabriel muttered as the whale-of-war kept diving.

Then he saw its sides expand. It leveled off. And it kept coming.

They were moving fast, buoyancy and the engines working together to rocket them up.

"Depth three hundred feet." Another proximity alarm rang out, clanging insistently over Peter's voice.

"Current speed?" Gabriel ran to the wall and smacked the proximity alarm to shut it up.

"Seventy knots. That's top speed right now—we're gonna burn out."

"Okay. Speed of the pursuer?"

"Sixty-eight knots." Peter looked up. "That thing is

swimming at seventy-eight miles an hour. Wait…" He consulted the screen. "Seventy-nine. It's speeding up."

How?

"Battle stations." Gabriel shook his head. He had never said the words before. "Misty, prepare weapons. Peter, activate the water mics. I want to hear it."

"Uh…okay." Misty sounded like she was racing to make the same transition Gabriel had, running through training they'd all been through but, honestly, had never taken all that seriously. She clicked her safety belts shut around her waist as she rattled off the systems. "Defensive measures online. Torpedoes?"

"Yes."

The water microphones came online then, and they heard the roar of water pushing around the pursuing creature. And more: the whining cry of the Lodger, warbling through the water.

"Pincer torpedoes…ready, you just have to tell me how powerful to set them."

"Seventy-two knots pursuing, Gabriel. Time to impact…" Peter calculated. "Sixty-five seconds."

"Open torpedo bay doors." Gabriel closed his eyes for a moment. *Breathe. Don't let the enemy in, and don't let your own mind get ahead of you.*

"We should fire," Peter insisted. "Maximum load, that'll probably be as powerful as a real torpedo."

"What? Maximum load could destroy it."

Peter pointed at the screen. "Gabe, *look* at that thing. Anything less isn't even going to slow it down. Can't you see that?"

"It's an *unknown biological*," Gabriel said through clenched teeth. "I can't be the first human to kill one of these creatures. I won't."

"Time to impact: forty-five seconds."

Misty spoke intently. "Gabe—you're *right*. They're a mystery, and it would be terrible. But you can't commit suicide because those creatures don't know who their friends are. *We* can't."

Would the creature try to punch through them? Or bite them? It was growing now, the sharp metal nose and grinning, toothy mouth wide. Its shrieking mixed with the roar of the water.

"Thirty seconds."

"Let's not start at World War Three," Gabriel said. "Okay? Not maximum."

"Would you just make up your mind?" Peter shouted. "You're lucky I don't blow it up *for* you."

Gabriel nodded dramatically. "I hear you. Okay. Electric warheads...fifty percent load. On my mark...."

"*Twenty-five* seconds."

"Fire."

Misty punched a button. "Torpedo away," she said, and a silvery missile that glowed with shimmering mother-of-pearl spun like a bullet through the water.

"Okay, that should distract it. Dive twenty meters!" Gabriel said.

Peter sent them lurching into a dive, and Gabriel staggered back to his seat, snapping on his safety belt. They leveled off as he kept his eye on the missile flying toward the gnarly teeth of the creature.

The torpedo impacted just below the prow. First, a ball of gas exploded all around it, obscuring the view. Then a cloud of electricity arced in the same ball, tendrils of energy dancing out of the explosion and sparking up and down the gnarled face. Pincer energy sizzled in the masts.

The creature slowed and Peter sped them up.

"Let's make distance," Gabriel said. "While it's still..."

The creature shook its great head back and forth and seemed to chuff, gases exploding from its sides. And then it started moving again.

The great teeth snapped as it lurched toward them.

"Oh boy, I think we made it mad," Peter said.

Gabriel shook his head. So that was it. Just like that, he had failed at everything his sister had asked. "Misty, let's take it out. Maximum load," he said dully. "Fire when ready."

"Ready," Misty said. Then she pushed the button.

Light flickered in the bridge and the engines roared, followed by a *chutting* sound.

No missile appeared on the screen. Just the pursuing monster.

"What happened?" Gabriel shouted.

"It's not firing!" Misty slapped the controls.

"Engines are choked with garbage, they're burning out, all power is diverting to the engines," Peter shouted rapidly. "I'm sorry, that means..."

"Weapons are offline," Misty said.

The bridge went dark for a second; then red auxiliary lights filled the room. The screen still flickered, weak and snowy. So they could see their own doom. The creature was charging fast.

Gabriel struck his forehead with his fists. *Heck of a ship you got here, Nemo.*

"Gabriel!" Peter shouted. "*Time to impact is eight seconds!*"

Gabriel opened his mouth to say the word *brace* when he heard a massive, churning engine roar and drown out the sound of the whale-of-war.

Peter shouted, "Captain, there's another—"

"*Obscure*," a female voice said, crackling to life over a speaker in the ceiling that Gabriel had never had occasion to use.

Gabriel looked up at the sound.

"Brace for wake," the voice said rapidly.

"Nerissa?"

She came up from below.

The nuclear-powered engines of a much bigger submarine roared and blasted over the speakers as a long, tapered nose sixty feet across came into view. The man-of-war was still closing, twisting upward to strike—it was going to bite them after all—when the nose of the *Nebula* smashed into the front of the man-of-war, battering it out of the way, bits of wood and metal flying through the water. The *Nebula* kept coming, soaring up past the *Obscure*'s cameras, its sides all shimmering with mother-of-pearl, its portholes sculpted in the same manner as the *Obscure*'s and even the long-lost *Nautilus*'s.

The wake of the impact sent them tumbling, and for a moment they were spinning. The *Obscure* pitched up on its side, and papers flew as the crew strained against their safety belts before systems kicked on, air hissing and stabilizer wings moving to right the ship.

"Report!" shouted Gabriel.

"Bulkheads secure, but we have damage to auxiliary ballast tanks and pumps from that tumble we took." Misty read her screen as fast as she could. "Batteries... are at twenty-five percent."

Peter added, "And engines are at fifteen percent. Man, this water is the pits for the engines."

The cameras had gone fuzzy until they were righted and then popped back. "Front cameras only," Gabriel ordered.

They were pointed in completely the opposite direction that they had been, and as the picture came back Gabriel caught the aft of the *Nebula* filling the screen and then disappearing fast above them.

Beyond, the water swirled with a cloud of detritus. Bits

of wood churned as if in a school of their own. Dust billowed like smoke in the distance.

"I don't hear the man-of-war. Magnify?"

"I don't see it."

Just dust. As far as the eye could see. The man-of-war could be dead or alive.

"*Obscure* to *Nebula*." The Nemotech intercom in the ceiling communicated directly with any other Nemotech ship. It was a privilege afforded to family only. "Come in, *Nebula*."

Nerissa came back after a moment "Hi, Gabe. We have some damage here. Are you all right?"

"Same..." Gabriel stopped, smiling so hard that he felt it in his eyes. "Same here."

"Meet us on the surface," Nerissa said. "There's been some developments."

13

THE SEA WAS calm when the *Obscure* joined the *Nebula* at the surface. The *Obscure*, dwarfed by its sister ship, lay shoulder to battering-ram nose, and the *Nebula* crew made quick work of extending a gangplank between the two.

As Misty joined Gabriel on the catwalk, she nodded at the *Nebula*. "So I get to meet the sister."

"Yeah, about that." He stopped. Maybe Nerissa was already watching. "There's this thing that I didn't mention."

"What's that?" Misty covered her face. "Does she have, like, one eye, like a pirate, and I'm not supposed to mention it? Because that would be awesome."

He couldn't believe she was making jokes so soon after he'd nearly gotten her killed. "Last I saw her, she had both eyes."

"Who's *this*?" Nerissa's voice boomed through a loud-speaker.

Gabriel winced. "She kinda doesn't know that I brought you guys."

"Whatever." Misty rolled her eyes and clambered along the catwalk toward the *Nebula*'s hatch. "You shocked out my hair; I'm gonna meet your sister."

A pair of *Nebula* crewmen met them at the hatch and led them down through the shining *Nebula* bridge. Misty looked around as they went and nodded at an open hatch into a corridor that seemed nearly as wide as the *Obscure* itself. "This ship could swallow us whole."

The crewmen led them into the captain's study and shut the door behind them. Nerissa's study was similar to the one that Gabriel had on the *Obscure*, but less obviously Victorian; there were shelves of dark coral-laced steel and rows of soft lights set in enormous, recessed clamshells. They found Nerissa standing next to a large porthole, her arms folded. In front of her was a table set with tea.

Nerissa wore a blue uniform that Gabriel remembered seeing on a drawing board once, not long before she took off on her own. It was wide at the shoulder, with gold braids and rank insignia, though Nerissa skipped the hat that everyone else in her crew wore.

Gabriel and Misty just stood there waiting for her to speak. Finally Gabriel folded his arms to match Nerissa's. "Well, this is nice."

"No crew."

"Come on," Gabriel said.

Nerissa pointed at the wall in the direction of the *Obscure*. "That thing could practically drive itself, and you . . . what did I tell you?"

"Hi." Misty extended a hand that hung there while Nerissa kept her eyes on Gabriel. "I'm Misty."

"This mission needs a crew." Gabriel shrugged. "I know what I'm doing."

"You said that you wouldn't—"

"I *said*," Gabriel responded, "that you would hear no more about it. This was a *Gabriel thing*, remember? And also you're not the boss of me."

Beside him, Misty seemed to roll her eyes with her entire body. "Really?"

Gabriel grunted. He was doing the best he could. He returned to meeting his sister's gaze. "But. Nerissa. Here you are, and thank you. I mean, really. We wouldn't have made it without you."

"Yeah, well, I *am* glad you're not Lodger food. And anyway, I put you in this mess." Nerissa looked down. "So, do Mom and Dad have any idea about . . . ?" She indicated Misty.

"They know all about them."

Nerissa scoffed. "If I ever talk to them, I'll find out if that's true." Then she politely offered her hand to Misty.

"Welcome aboard the *Nebula*. Beware, you're now in the world of wanted men. I'm Nerissa."

"Misty," she said again

"Why don't you sit?" Nerissa sighed, then went to the tea set and began pouring cups out of a silver pot. "So *you're* the crew."

"There's one more. Peter is at the helm." Gabriel tapped his earpiece.

"I like your study." Misty swept her arm around the room. "Gabriel has one just like it, almost. A little less cool."

"Thanks," both Nemos responded, Gabriel with considerably less sincerity.

"We call it the Outer Sanctum," Nerissa said. "This tea service is something you'd appreciate, Gabriel—we pulled it from the wreck of the *Yamato*."

The *Yamato* was a large Japanese battle cruiser sunk during World War II. And she was right; that was pretty cool.

She handed a cup to each of them, the steam rising to their faces. "Now, this tea is a Nemo strain. Completely sea-drawn." Nerissa turned to Gabriel as he lifted his cup and sipped. It was slightly sweet and salty, and he felt warmth travel through his torso as he drank. "Anyway. I'm pretty sure you would have done the same for me."

Gabriel shook his head. "With the *Obscure*? Forget it.

Did you see that thing before you rammed it? It was a British man-of-war. Literally." He held his hands apart just to illustrate sheer bigness.

"Yeah, don't tell the crew, but it's the biggest one I've ever seen."

Gabriel heard this and threw Misty a look that said, *I promise I'm not like that.*

Don't tell the crew something's wrong. That was sort of a rule. Don't ever say *I can't believe it* or *I've never seen anything like this* in front of the crew. Nerissa had learned and believed that admitting something like that would freak out the people you were leading. Gabriel knew all those rules, but he was replacing them with his own. His crew *needed* to know what he was thinking. And besides: They were his friends.

"Since the B-17 I saw, we've run into a few little submarines and some downed fighter jets. But they didn't get close. Other than the man-of-war, what about you?" Nerissa asked.

"Nothing until we got to the Garbage Patch." Gabriel put down his teacup. He wished his sister had offered them soda instead. "But get this: The first one we saw was out of its shell."

"Really? What did it look like?"

"We didn't get a good look. It was trying to put on an old fishing trawler that was adrift. We saw tentacles and a head...like a crawfish, basically."

132

"And it attacked you. Just like the man-of-war did."

Misty cleared her throat and chimed in, "I'm not sure *attacked* is the right word. We happened to be in the wrong place at the wrong time. I think we *disturbed* it, the one that was, you know, naked, basically. One of the tentacles trapped me, and Gabe shocked it with his pincer gun. That ticked off a second Lodger that was swimming nearby as though... it was like it was standing guard."

"Right," Gabriel agreed. "*Right.* That one was a *biplane.* When we got in the naked one's way, it came after us. Then it chased us into the water and another joined in. Then the big one came along."

"Okay." Nerissa stood up, massaging her neck. "The B-17 just jumped over us. The fighter jets, too—they flew by underwater. But what you're describing is something like... pod behavior."

"Like killer whales?" Gabriel asked.

Misty said, "Right. They'll even split up and try to cause diversions to keep whalers confused."

"Which means... I don't know." Nerissa thought for a moment. "Maybe we can communicate with them?"

"We can barely communicate with whales," Gabriel observed.

"Pod behavior. So far we've seen loners, twos, now three—"

"And this water is thick with garbage. It fouls up sonar and cuts visibility. There's no telling what we didn't see."

"Argh." Nerissa collapsed into her chair. "What *are* they? Are they crabs of some kind? Crabs don't hang out in pods."

"What's important is that they don't seem prone to attack unless provoked. Maybe you can tell the navy..."

"We don't know they aren't prone to attack." Misty opened her hands. And she was right, Gabriel realized. They were making a lot of guesses. "How do the Lodgers know if a ship is empty? If it's on the bottom of the ocean, it's no problem, but *we* were on that trawler."

"Yeah, *why* were you on a trawler again?" Nerissa asked.

"Search and rescue."

"Okay," Nerissa grumbled. "Gabe, you're going to get yourself killed."

"*You* sent me on this mission." Gabriel smirked. "And by the way, Nerissa, you haven't told us. Why are *you* here? This was supposed to be—"

"A Gabriel thing, I know." She rubbed her forehead. "But it's gotten worse."

"Gabe?" Peter's voice came in Gabriel's earpiece, and he held up a hand as Misty indicated with a nod that she was getting the same message. Gabriel touched a button on his earpiece and set it on the table, and Peter's voice burst from a small speaker. "Are you there?"

"Go ahead."

"We've picked up a...straggler."

"What do you mean?"

"We got one of those things chewing on the starboard forward camera gear. I think it's…I think it was the biplane."

"Comms," Nerissa called to her bridge. "Release a Bubo and send it to the starboard prow of the *Obscure*. Let me see it in the OS."

"*Bubo*?" Misty asked. "What's that?"

"It's a drone," Gabriel said. "It has cameras."

"She calls the drones Bubo?"

"*Clash of the Titans*," both the Nemos answered. That was one of the mythology movies they had watched a lot. The hero had a robot owl that came in pretty handy.

An image flickered on the screen in the Sanctum and they were in the little drone, flying through water toward the *Obscure*.

"There it is." On the screen, a creature that looked vaguely like a squid with the head of a crawfish had grabbed onto the camera gear sticking out of the *Obscure*'s side. The creature was about twenty feet long, with tentacles up and down its length—and dangling off the end were the battered remains of the biplane, the landing gear and a piece of the wing.

"It must have been damaged when you came up, Nerissa," Gabriel said. He stared at it. "But *now* what is it up to?"

The final piece of the biplane fell away as the creature slapped itself up against the hull of the *Obscure*. Two of its tentacles extended frond hands and began to glow, sending gaseous bubbles in the water.

"*No no no!*" Gabriel found himself reaching out toward the screen. "It's gonna try to burn through the hull."

Misty clapped a hand over her mouth. "We need to get if off the ship. Peter's still on board; it could tear the ship apart."

"Peter, are you seeing this?" Gabriel asked.

"Heck *yes*, I'm seeing it."

"Options." Gabriel looked around the room, but he was including Peter as well. "I'll start. We can't shoot it with a torpedo, even a nonlethal one. Mine wouldn't be able to hit my own hull and even if they did, one mistake and I could accidentally punch a hole through the *Obscure*."

"Hull integrity ninety-eight percent," Peter reported. "It's burning slowly, but it's burning."

"Peter, if there's a breach I need you down there to shore it up double-time."

Peter paused. "Aye."

"We won't let it come to that, though. More options."

"We can just . . . *yank* it off," Nerissa offered. "I can send a team in a small craft with spades and hooks and physically pull it away."

"No, no." Gabriel watched the creature. "No. If we're pulling it away it'll just grab us again." He thought. It was true it would try to grab onto the hull again. But he realized that maybe they had gotten lucky after all. At least if they moved fast enough to avoid too much damage. "I think we have an opportunity here." He turned to Misty. "Let's go *fishing*."

"Fishing?" Nerissa asked. "You're talking about *capturing* it?"

"Absolutely. You said yourself that we need to know more about them. We could..."

"Eatin' away at the hull over here, guys." Peter sounded alarmed now.

"Where are you going to put it?" Nerissa demanded. "It's twenty feet long. You'd need a tank thirty feet by, what, fifteen? Even I can't fit that. You gonna put it in your passenger compartment?"

"*No*, come on." This could work. Gabriel started walking, Misty following him out of the captain's study and into the corridor toward the ladder they'd used to get in. "We encase the Lodger in nets, hard metal nets. We've both got them. And then we *haul* it."

"Haul it where?" Nerissa demanded.

"You *know* where."

"Now *you* come on." Nerissa stopped him, her eyes wide and imploring. He wasn't used to his sister showing any kind of vulnerability, and even this hint of it made him desperately sorry and uncomfortable. "You know I can't go back there," she said.

He liked thinking of his sister as a kind of brilliant tyrant who had been telling him what to do for as long as he could remember. He wasn't ready for *vulnerable* Nerissa. And he knew that if it were him whining like that, she'd bite his head off.

"Okay," Gabriel said. "Well, you do what you need to. I've got a ship in trouble. Peter? Misty and I are coming back so we can prepare some nets."

"I already told you I could use a team to save your ship." Nerissa's voice returned to its flat, hard insistence. "This is absolutely not what I asked you to do. You're going to risk your middle schooler friends *again*?"

Gabriel held up a defiant finger. "We're a *crew*. It's *my* ship. If anyone's doing this operation, we are."

"Do *you* have," Nerissa growled, turning to Misty, "any idea what you're doing? Has he given you the training that you need to go capture a twenty-foot sea creature? Because I'm betting there's no amount of training that can ready you for all of this."

Misty seemed brought up short by that—she made as if to speak and then looked away.

"She's trained." Gabriel got between them. "Now come on, this is wasting time. Are you going to help us, or am I running all the way back to my ship to get my own equipment?"

"Guys?" Peter squawked. "As awesome as the Nemo Family Reality Show is, that thing won't be stopped by the outer hull for long."

Nerissa scowled. "All right. Helm? Deploy towing cable, one hundred yards, slack." She turned to Gabriel. "Let's get some nets."

Nerissa's dive room was situated at the bottom of the *Nebula* roughly halfway to the tail. She stopped them as they reached a dimly lit room with a series of lockers. Nerissa found the locker she was looking for and used her palm to open it. After it swung open, Nerissa grabbed three harpoon guns, two of which she rapidly handed to Gabriel and Misty, keeping one for herself. Next she handed out three special, round harpoon heads about the size of cantaloupes.

"Fasten these to the harpoons." Nerissa locked the harpoon head she held onto the end of her harpoon gun. They copied her movements. She tossed them rebreathers. They put the cords around their necks, and Nerissa turned to Misty. "You ever use these?"

"All the time." Misty's voice sounded slightly cold.

Nerissa shook her head and muttered something, then opened another locker and pulled out three thick diving hoods and goggles. "Hoods. Keep your goggles secure to your hood, because just a few meters down and it gets really cold out here. You'll go blind and very probably die."

"I've actually heard that speech," Misty called as they ran into the dive room.

"I don't care if you've heard it." Nerissa hit a switch on

the wall, and the dive room began to fill with water. She glared at Gabriel. "I care if you *listen*."

Gabriel breathed. He wanted to scream at his sister. And he would. Just not now. Not now. She seemed to be letting her own anger get in the way of the mission in a way she'd never forgive someone else for. He'd never seen her so angry.

"Nerissa. This is my op. It's my ship we're saving, so when we hit the water, we follow my calls. All right?" Gabriel spoke through his mic calmly, going a little overboard to provide the opposite of Nerissa's mood. Cold water came up past his neck. "We'll have one shot."

The Nemo suits kept their skin warm as Gabriel started swimming away from the body of the *Nebula* toward the forward hull of the *Obscure*. Hooked to a belt around his waist was a heavy metal hook attached to a slack cable that extended all the way back to the *Nebula*. Misty and Nerissa swam not far on either side of him, holding their harpoon rifles before them and kicking steadily.

Up ahead they could see the cone of bright yellow-white light from the exterior lamps. Below that they saw the creature, partially wrapped under the hull. They hung in the water for a moment watching it.

Gabriel wondered how the former biplane creature had lost its shell. Maybe the whale-of-war had collided with it when Nerissa knocked into it. It was still giant, as long as a full-grown whale, its crawfishlike head the size of a refrigerator. The burning little appendages on the fronds of its tentacles gave off a warm red glow against the *Obscure*'s hull.

"Try not to touch it." They swam closer as slowly as possible, barely kicking. Gabriel had no idea how sensitive the creature was, whether it could smell them like a shark or sense vibrations a mile away—it was a long column of unknown-unknown-unknown in the checklist of aquatic capabilities.

"Dive team, I see you," Peter said in his ear.

"Copy. Team, you ready to move?"

"Ready," they responded.

The first thing Gabriel noticed as they got closer to the creature was the humming.

As it swayed slowly, it made a sound similar to the screeching he had heard on the trawler, but less angry, more a hum, almost like singing. Gabriel couldn't help but think of the noise as plaintive. For a brief moment he felt guilt over capturing the thing. But it needed to be done.

"You go around." Gabriel pointed to Nerissa. "Get on the other side. I'll go under toward its head. Misty, stay on this side. Box it in."

Nerissa started swimming, using slow, tiny strokes, moving out beyond the creature, who was sticking close to the cone of light. After she'd gone far past the creature's position, she checked in with an "Okay."

Gabriel meanwhile was moving below it, down and close to the skin of the *Obscure*.

"Okay," Gabriel said. "Go."

Misty pulled her trigger. There was a little explosion of air at the end of her gun, and the harpoon traveled faster than the eye could follow, but he could see the silvery line trailing it. The harpoon traveled about twenty yards over the top of the creature until it was beyond it. Then the ball head on the harpoon burst in the water, hundreds of little weights spreading out in a spiderweb pattern and falling over the creature.

Gabriel swam below the creature and pointed up. He needed the net to explode upward, to get the net to expand around as much of the Lodger from below as possible, because the creature was still working away and attached to the hull. He pulled the trigger and fired, the harpoon traveling past the head and exploding, the netting flying away around the head.

Nerissa, on the other side, fired toward Misty's side, the net falling around the back half of the creature.

"Fall back!" Gabriel shouted.

As soon as the nets started to fall, the creature began to warble loudly. Its cry shot through the water and it reared up, the whole squidlike body twisting. Gabriel swam backward, moving aside as hundreds of small magnetic ends from all three nets fell down through the water and found one another, encasing the creature like a mummy. The

Lodger began flailing and getting caught in the netting. Gabriel felt pretty confident it would hold. The netting was reinforced with steel and would not break unless the Lodger could burn through the whole thing.

Pretty confident. The creature turned its head toward him, a head bigger than Gabriel's body, its teeth glimmering inside its working mandibles. Its stalk eyes locked onto him through the netting, and its tentacles began to whip fast as it tried to swim straight for him.

"*Gyahh*, it's trying to grab me!" he cried. Even with those teeth behind a metal net, he didn't like being snapped at. "I'm gonna attach the line and then we're out of here."

Gabriel swam away from the head as the creature reached through the net with a tentacle, chasing him as he held out the shiny hook. He reached a point halfway down its body and lunged with the hook.

The thing bucked, whipping against him, and the cable fell away. "I dropped it!"

"Going after it." Misty dove for the cable as it fell toward her. Past the lunging creature, he saw Misty dart down, chasing the silver line.

"I'm loading a trawling line," Nerissa said. On the other side of the creature, she slid a harpoon into her gun and fired.

"Don't shoot it!"

"Trust me." The harpoon flew right underneath the netting over the creature's back and snagged in the net, and instantly Nerissa was yanked in the water by the line at the end. She held on to the gun as it twisted in the water.

The creature dipped its head down, the stalk eyes finding Gabriel again, and it tried to bite him through the net, lunging.

"Where's the line?" Nerissa shouted.

"Coming." Misty swam fast toward her.

Gabriel swam back as rapidly as he could as the teeth lunged at him through the net, and he heard a mechanical humming sound. Nerissa was using the reel on her harpoon gun, trying to pull at it, to no effect.

Gabriel swam up around the head, trying to get away from the teeth. He saw the burning appendages on the frond hand that had been on the hull come away and swipe at Nerissa. It snagged her right on the goggles, and she yelped.

"*Argh.* I can't see." Nerissa swam back, cursing as she yanked the burning goggles away.

"Hang on, hang on!" Gabriel called, swimming toward her.

"I've got the line," Misty's voice crackled, and in his peripheral view he saw her hook the silver line into the net at the back of the creature. "Nerissa, are you all right?"

"Keep your eyes closed!" Gabriel called as he swam. "Everyone get clear. Nerissa, I'm coming." His sister was in trouble. He reached out his hands, begging himself to close the gap faster.

Nerissa kicked toward her ship with her hand over her eyes, dropping the harpoon gun and shouting as she went. "*Nebula*, take in the slack, three hundred yards and hold!"

"Copy," came a voice from the *Nebula*.

Gabriel reached Nerissa, putting his arm under hers. The creature started moving fast as the line reeled it back. The slack was gone. "Come on, we're going," he said to Nerissa. "I've got you."

They started to swim along the line, away from the creature that was still screaming and pulling, for naught. Misty fell in next to them.

"Let's get inside." He guided his sister by the shoulder as she kicked, her eyes closed the whole time. "Don't look now. But that's a heck of a ship you've got there."

"Yeah, you're loving this."

"You know he is," Misty agreed.

Gabriel kept swimming with his arm around Nerissa. Misty looked over at him and gave him a silent thumbs-up as they reached the iris into the *Nebula*'s dive room.

They had captured a Lodger.

14

IN THE DIMLY lit engine room tucked below the passenger compartment of the *Obscure*, Gabriel lay on his back and opened up one panel after another. Misty crouched next to him with a flashlight as Gabriel used a brush to scrape mounds of plastic pellets out of the machinery.

"Ugh," Gabriel said. "Hand me that skinnier brush."

Misty handed him a different brush as she spoke to the bridge. "Peter, how's the Lodger?"

Peter came back, "Stuck pretty well. If he's figuring out how to escape, he hasn't let us know yet."

"Hey, we have no idea if it's a *he*," Gabriel said as he dislodged a bunch of pellets and let them drop in a thick mound next to his head.

Right now the creature was suspended between the

two ships in its net, and as soon as the *Obscure* had cleaned out its engines, they would all be on their way. He had already poured a thinner into the system that should keep it from fouling up again—if they were lucky and didn't overtax the engines. But the garbage in the *Obscure*'s gears still meant that Gabriel had to spend an hour on his back under a choked machine.

"How come your sister's engines didn't get clogged up?"

Gabriel shut the panel before him and worked his shoulders, sliding over a foot and a half to open another. He peered in, seeing more masses of wet, goopy plastic. He sighed and started brushing it out. "We're just smaller. The *Obscure* converts seawater into energy, but the filters aren't fine enough to deal with this stuff, and our engines are small enough that they get choked. The *Nebula* doesn't have that problem." He looked up at Misty, who kept the flashlight trained on the panel. "But then, who knows, maybe they did get fouled up and she didn't mention it to us."

"So would your sister be stuck mucking out her own engine?"

Gabriel laughed. "She has people for everything."

Misty shifted her weight from one heel to the other. "Where does she get them all? Her crew, I mean."

"I have no idea." It was the truth. "The original Captain Nemo built his crew from guys who knew the sea and were sick of their own navies. I guess she's pretty much the same."

"Can there really be hundreds of people ready to pledge to follow to one woman on a wanted ship?"

"That ship and *that* woman?" He shrugged. "People follow crazy."

"That's gotta be true," Misty said. "Hey, can I ask you something?"

"Shoot." He closed the panel. He was about to call for Peter to test the engines when he looked up to see concern on Misty's face. "What is it?"

"Do you trust my opinion?"

"I . . . of course I do. What kinda question is that?"

"I just wonder."

"Okay," he said. He knew he'd lost her respect. It served him right. "I didn't know all this plastic would clog up the engines. But we're gonna get going."

"I get it. You call the shots. You line them up, we throw out ideas, and you pick one. We throw out ideas; you call the shots. That's how we do it."

"Okay."

"Even if you're wrong."

"I mean, that's how a chain of command works, but . . . what are you saying?"

She touched her chin with her hand, still holding the flashlight, so that the beam lost its place for a moment before she brought it back. "I want to say something *is* wrong. It was something Nerissa said, which I've been thinking about."

"Listen, I grew up with her, and I'd throw myself in a volcano for her, but don't let her get in your head."

"I think you only say that because you know what Nerissa said was true," Misty said. "I have to tell you. I think this is it for me."

A moment of panic flooded through him and caught him off guard. "What?"

"Gabriel, we're *lying*, outright lying, to our parents. And it has been amazing. We saved all those people on the burning ship and didn't tell anyone. It was *fun*. And I get that it was dangerous. But this..."

"Look, I know the creature on the ship was a surprise."

"You have literally no idea what you sound like to us." Her bushy brows furrowed. "You *expect* to throw yourself into danger like it's your life's calling, and I guess it is. And you don't know that that's a lot to ask of us."

"I...I get that." That made sense. Of course. He was asking these people to risk their lives. For a good cause, one he himself had been serving his whole life. "Maybe it's too much to ask."

"No, I'm not afraid for myself. I mean, I am, but I'm an action girl. But the thing is, I could have *died* out there on the boat when you saved me, and no one would have known where I was. My parents would never know that I was thousands of miles away in open sea. That's what's not fair. You've taken us on the most dangerous mission we've ever done, and if you don't mind me saying so, probably the most dangerous mission *you've* ever done."

"We can make sure you don't do anything you can't handle."

"Who decides that? You and me and Peter, who can't *swim?*"

He had to surrender. There was no way around what she was saying. This was more dangerous than he'd suggested at first, and she wasn't even being cowardly about it. She was being loyal. Loyal to her family. He had to respect that. "Okay. I hear you."

"Then hear this: Your sister is right. I'll help you get this creature somewhere we can study it. But this is it. This is my last secret."

Gabriel nodded. "I don't mean for you to…" But he didn't know where to go with that. "I understand." He shut the panel before him. It would probably do for now.

He wanted to carry on the conversation with Misty, but what was he going to say? *No, I promise, everything from here on out will be a snap.* Or what was really under all of that: *I can't do this alone. I can't go back to that little house and be alone.*

He called Peter. "Okay, let's start her up."

Soon enough, the engines started humming and Gabriel stood, following Misty up a short ladder into the passenger compartment. He was glad to be moving. It was as though Misty had pushed him to the edge of his ability to converse.

He looked out a porthole at the net suspended between the two subs. The creature occupied a mass of netting in the center, looking rather like an egg. It had stopped fighting.

"Now I guess we gotta take it home," he said.

"Home?" Misty asked.

"*My* home. We have to take it to Nemolab."

15

"*NEBULA*?" GABRIEL RAISED his head, looking at the intercom in the ceiling.

"Plotting course for the Dakkar Curtain," Nerissa answered.

Peter looked up. "The what?"

"It's the gateway to the valley where you'll find Nemolab." Gabriel gave him the coordinates. "Keep us steady with the *Nebula* so that the net remains suspended safely between us."

"Aye. Okay, time to arrival twelve hours."

"Copy." Gabriel looked at Misty and Peter. "You've never come this far. But Nemolab is hidden for a reason. The good thing is once we're underway, I think we should divide the time up into miniwatches and everyone can get a few hours' sleep. Uh...is everyone good with that?"

"You're asking us *now?*" Peter smirked.

"I know I could use some sleep," Misty said. "And you two could, too."

"Yeah," Gabriel said. "No kidding. Okay, let's mind our stations. Peter?"

"Aye."

"Prepare to dive. Next stop, Nemolab."

The two ships dove deep in caravan, the *Nebula* in the lead and the *Obscure* off her starboard side. Schools of fish darted like clouds in the distance, and occasionally they saw the edge of great pods of whales.

Deeper and farther the Nemoships flew.

Over the next half day, the crew of the *Obscure* slept, and watched, and slept. They saw flickering fields of half-buried jewelry lost to ancient crews. They saw sculptures of guardians hewn by unknown hands, standing at unremembered caverns measureless to man. They saw a mound of tombstones that had slid from a cargo ship in 1972 and landed on the seafloor, many of the stones upright, forming an instant and undiscovered graveyard. They saw waves of jellyfish and glowing silver creatures, spindly unnamable things and ancient turtles. They saw mountain after mountain as they dove and traveled and discovered.

And then Gabriel told Peter to be wary, because the trench was drawing near.

They dropped into a new cavern with mountains on either side.

"This is the Dakkar Trench." Gabriel pointed to the wall of rock on their right and waited for a thin crack to pass. *Dakkar*, after the original name of his ancestor. As they passed the crack in the wall, Gabriel could see a tiny red light shimmering in the shadows. "And we just passed a perimeter alarm."

They moved on for miles in the shadows of the undersea mountains until finally they saw a natural rock formation, a series of very high columns: the Dakkar Curtain. It rose like a rocky grate across the trench, seventy feet high, seven pillars separated by about thirty feet of clearance.

"Nerissa, go ahead and detach the net on your side. We'll haul the creature ourselves the rest of the way." It wasn't far now.

"Detaching net," Nerissa replied. Outside, the *Nebula* let go of its end of the net, and the creature slid in the water until it was trailing behind the *Obscure* as the *Nebula* continued ahead of them.

∿∿

"How is Nerissa going to get through that?" Misty stood next to Gabriel at the view screen. Up ahead, the *Nebula* had slowed.

"Watch," Gabriel said.

"Approaching curtain." Nerissa's voice crackled on the intercom, and they saw the *Nebula* begin to tilt, farther and farther on its starboard side.

The *Nebula* moved forward, tilted almost to ninety degrees, and sailed in, rock sliding by the silvery skin of the submarine, close enough to kiss.

"I'll bet everyone's hanging off their seats," Peter said.

"Sometimes." Gabriel watched as the *Nebula* cleared the curtain. "Our turn. Tilt a little just to be safe."

Peter slowed the *Obscure* and they entered the Dakkar Curtain, the high gray columns greeting them on each side. Once they were through, a choice lay ahead—they could stay up to travel in the canyon that seemed to go on forever, or they could dip and dive down into the wide mouth of a tunnel.

Gabriel said, "Dive into the tunnel." Up ahead, the *Nebula* dove first, slipping down and disappearing into darkness.

"Diving, aye," Peter repeated, and they dipped, slipping after the *Nebula* into the hole in the bottom of the ocean. Soon they leveled into a long natural tunnel under the floor of the canyon. On the view screen, the tunnel ceiling groped for them with stalactites.

"Steady as she goes, Peter. Keep at least fifty feet between us and the top or the bottom."

Misty was looking at her screen. "I've got a visual on

the Lodger. He's wriggling around but not really veering anywhere. Steady."

After another mile, they emptied out of the tunnel and a wide shelf of seafloor stretched out beyond them. Ahead, Nerissa's *Nebula* disappeared into a cloud. A moment later, the screen filled with waves of dust and silt.

"Visual zero percent." Peter looked at Gabriel. "It might be a little dangerous to maintain this course. Even sonar won't work."

"Push through."

The *Obscure* proceeded, and then the ship rumbled with the pressure of hydraulic nozzles kicking up silt from the ocean floor.

Gabriel felt his chest tightening with anticipation. He could feel it now, before he could even see it. They moved through the cloud blind and, when they emerged on the other side, Gabriel was home.

The billows of sand drifted away, and Gabriel's heart caught in his throat. The shelf they flew over ran another hundred yards, and then as they slipped over the edge, a great valley opened up below. Mountains rose on both sides, teeming with deepwater reefs and schools of manta rays. And in between the two mountains, filling a flat expanse four thousand feet wide, was the complex known as Nemolab.

The *Obscure* dropped off the shelf and leveled out as a circular landing strip began pulsing with bright, faintly pink-and-green strobes. The *Nebula* would not fit there and would need to anchor near the other landing pad now lighting up at the far-right end of the complex.

"Steady as she goes, Peter," said Gabriel.

Peter stared, then shook his head, turning back to the controls. "Steady, aye, headed for the landing pad."

Misty's voice came from over Gabriel's shoulder. "Goodness."

After the strobing landing pad, the next thing to catch the eye was the Central Tower. At the tower's base was a geodesic dome a thousand feet across, nearly the size of the Pentagon, a perfect half globe of Nemoglass and mother-of-pearl. Inside, he could see familiar robots scurrying down corridors and leafy vegetables swaying in artificial winds in his mother's greenhouse.

From the top of the dome, a tower rose fifty feet wide and two hundred feet high, up to a sloped and flattened structure at the top from which a nest of antennae erupted. The tower was called the Manta, after the ray.

Protruding from the bottom, where manta rays dipped and dived around the glass, long tubes ran to other, smaller structures. There were domes of glass and shining mineral like the main one, smaller domes of shimmering metal, and a wide, long tentlike structure where vehicles were stored and repaired, as well as tubes in the landing path where ships could be attached and accessed by repair crews.

"I can't believe you grew up here." Misty seemed enraptured by the vision of the domes.

"Sometimes I can't, either."

Now, as the *Obscure* approached, Gabriel could see a ring of light around the tower.

"*Obscure.*" A new voice came on the loudspeaker. Gabriel looked and found a vaulted window at the very front of the dome, facing them, where two people stood. His mother and father, little figures in white smocks, waved at him, and he once again felt that throat-catching feeling. In fact, it had not gone away, and now he wondered if it ever would.

His mom was speaking. "Welcome home." His mom! He'd had no *idea* how much he missed them.

"I see you!" Gabriel spoke into the intercom, the one that would come online between any two Nemo receivers. He waved excitedly before realizing he was practically jumping up and down. He stole a glance at Peter, who was grinning at him. He laughed. Sue him; he was happy to be back here.

Then he thought of the net they were trailing. They needed to deal with the captured Lodger before anything else. He scanned across Nemolab until he saw an enormous dome at the edge of the biosynthetics lab that they used for treating schools of giant fish and other large creatures.

"Mom!" he shouted. "We've got a sample. A big one.

Request permission to dock and then get right to setting it up in the large study dome."

"Absolutely," came her voice, with its slight, partly French lilt.

"We'll need drones," Nerissa said.

16

IT SEEMED TO take forever to get the Lodger situated, though it was really only about thirty minutes. But Gabriel was aching to see his parents, to smell their clothes and feel their hugs, and every minute crept by painfully. Moving the netted Lodger into place required a small vessel similar to the *Obscure*'s escape dinghy to haul it into the vast dome. They used drones to create an entry point by removing seventeen large Nemoglass panels that connected to one another on one side of the dome and slotted together so smoothly that the seams were invisible. When the Lodger rested on the silt at the bottom of the dome, it had thirty feet of clearance all around. Then drones flew up with the Nemoglass sections, closing the creature in except for one small exit slot for Gabriel and Nerissa.

Then came the hardest part. Nerissa and Gabriel swam around the great creature and touched special poles to the net, and with an electric *pop*, the magnets holding the net together reversed themselves, and the net dropped like a curtain to the dome floor. The Lodger, instantly free, swung around slowly and locked its great stalk eyes on Gabriel as he swam down toward the last open panel in the dome.

The Lodger was sluggish at first, as if its captivity had lulled it into a kind of trance, which was something Gabriel had seen in other large creatures. But now it began to swim toward them as they hurried out through the panel, past floating drones that zipped around the Nemo siblings, fastening the panel in place.

Nerissa swam ahead around the dome until she was a shape beyond the refraction of the glass curve. Gabriel stopped and turned around, looking through the glass. The creature swam back and forth like a shark. Gabriel swam around the dome, giving a little wave to the *Obscure* where it rested clamped to the access tube on the landing pad.

He spoke into his mask. Finally! "Guys," he said, "let's meet my parents."

~~~

Once, when Gabriel was eight years old, a Nobel Prize winner had come to Nemolab. An African with a closely trimmed white beard and a dark suit, the man had arrived in a Swedish UN science submarine to talk about oceanic environmental issues with his parents. Gabriel had stayed in the corner of the room when the man arrived, but he watched intently. He remembered most the way the man moved—smoothly, dolphinlike, with a minimum of fuss. He had shaken each of their hands with a nod and a practiced, perfectly polite but not overly excited smile.

Gabriel wanted to be like that. He had really intended to play it cool. To meet his parents and shake their hands like a visiting Nobel Prize winner, big enough for all this, big enough for anything that came along. *Hello*, he would say. *Cool* like that.

All of that melted away the moment he heard the tube from the landing pad attach itself to the dive room hatch.

Gabriel turned to Misty and Peter. "Follow me." He slid down the metal tube before the locks were finished whirring into place.

He ran past the engineers at the bottom of the ladder and along the corridor, his feet echoing in the underground tunnel. He bounded up a wide flight of stairs where the corridor to the other pad was emptying out, hearing rapid footsteps from that direction as well. Up through an iris that opened as soon as the circuitry in his collar came close, and up another flight.

He leapt into the receiving room with the big glass window, a wide wall of glass that looked out on the whole valley and its creatures, as well as the *Obscure* and the *Nebula*.

Before the glass were a man and a woman, both with jet-black hair and white coveralls, the man only a few inches taller than the woman.

The Drs. Yasmeen and David Nemo. His parents.

Gabriel threw himself into his mother's arms as his father wrapped himself around both of them somehow.

His mom ran her fingers through his hair and held him at a distance for a second, then repeated, "Welcome home."

He cleared his throat. He felt giddy being able to see her in person. Sure, he realized, that sounded like something a much smaller kid would feel. But he didn't care. He was even giddy at the smell of the air, which was slightly scented with rose petals. That was a touch from his mother. She had grown up on land before marrying his father, and she had brought new ideas and textures—and smells—to the Life Obscure.

"And who's this?" his father asked. Unlike his mom, his dad's accent was neutral, a little odd, as if he came from nowhere. Which was in fact the case.

Gabriel turned around to see Misty and Peter at the bottom of the wide staircase.

"Oh, yeah, sure." How stupid, he'd forgotten to introduce them. He still felt like he was bouncing out of his boots. He gestured crazily, waving his arms for his crew to come up. "Misty Jensen, she's my second and systems. Peter Kosydar, navigation."

"You're both welcome! We have plenty of room." Mom looked at them, and there was a little bit of a laugh in her voice. As if she were a little shocked that he had actually brought a couple of land-dwelling middle schoolers to the bottom of the ocean. Then she grew more serious. "But I know this isn't really a social visit."

Can't it be? thought Gabriel. *Can't we drop the experiment for a week or two, can't we go walking on the seafloor and study the volcanic vents, camp out under living mushrooms the size of football stadiums, watch the iridescent colors of creatures unknown to man as they parade past our faceplates? Can't it be social?*

"It's not," came the voice of Nerissa, and now the whole crew looked down to see her standing at the base of the entry stairs. Once more she had materialized like a ghost.

Mom sighed and opened her hands. Her eyes crinkled and misted.

Nerissa stood with her feet planted squarely, her arms held at her sides as though she wasn't sure what to do with them. "It's *not* social. Mom, please understand I wouldn't have risked your lab by bringing the *Nebula* here unless it was vital. The thing is, there's been a development," Nerissa explained. "We've intercepted calls from the US Navy. They're planning a large operation to find and destroy the Lodgers. This is planned for two days from *now*."

Gabriel watched his mom's eyes and thought he saw what she wanted to say. Especially to Nerissa, which had to be something like *You were wrong to run away*, and also *No, no, the risk is worth it, we will stand with you against whatever comes, and the burdens you take on yourself are too much for one person.*

But instead she said, "Then we'd better take a look at this sample of yours." And then she shook her head. "But I'm just so happy to see you. Both of you. *All* of you."

It was a nice enough greeting considering the madness that had ensued the morning Nerissa ran away from Nemolab.

That was a bad morning. He didn't like to think about it. He'd seen her from one of the big windows in the corridors, or at least seen the *Nebula*, starting up, lights erupting on the ocean floor around it. He'd called to her, shouting into the mic as he ran to the access tube, only to find the iris locked. She was leaving, and she was taking the *Nebula*. Leaving him when she was the only one he trusted to even *try* to understand this world his parents had made and the outside world they both yearned to see. She had taken the *Nebula* and *left* him.

It was a dark memory that made his heart ache. And as far as Gabriel knew, this was Nerissa's first time back.

It was his dad, though, who walked down the steps and took his daughter in his arms, then stepped back and looked from Nerissa to Gabriel. "You should know that

Mr. Zinoman thinks you're crazy, Gabriel." He leaned in, whispering loudly. "I think he's a little *afraid* of you."

The crew gathered at a large window in a corridor wall right at the bottom edge of the observation dome. They looked out on the creature as it swam up to the top of its near-invisible cage, feeling around with its tentacles, and back down. It hung near the bottom, close to the mirror window. Its stalk eyes staring as its tentacles moved it closer to the glass, where it floated, feeling all around and inspecting with slippery thoroughness the Nemoglass in front of it.

"Can it see us?" Peter asked.

"No—not with conventional chromatic vision, anyway. This is a one-way mirror." Gabriel's mom held up her hands to the window.

"Chromatic...?" Misty asked.

"That's the way we see," Mom said. "But who knows? Maybe it sees thermal signatures, too. Maybe it uses a type of sonar. We don't know."

"So it sees its own reflection right now?" Gabriel asked.

"Yes, and it's not acting like it sees an enemy or another creature," his mom observed. "I spent a semester watching dolphins react to mirrors. *They* knew it wasn't another creature, too. They tried to figure out the mirror, but they knew it was an illusion."

"So it's a little smart," Misty observed. "I've read about those dolphin experiments."

"Smart and dangerous." Peter nodded. "That thing was

trying to eat the *Obscure* when Gabriel, Misty, and Nerissa went out after it. It can put up a fight."

"It's in any creature's nature to defend itself," Mom said. "What sort of damage have they done?"

"Apparently they damaged a US Navy tender ship," Nerissa said. "I have no idea if the ship provoked them."

A two-way microphone and speaker beside the mirror broadcast sounds from inside the dome. Gabriel heard shuffling sounds as it moved its tentacles along the silty floor.

Abruptly the creature whined, its tentacles trembling in all directions as it hung in the middle of the tank. The whining rose and fell in pulses, dulled by the glass partition. It thrummed, sustained, and then relieved, repeating several times before stopping.

Misty said, "They all do that."

"But it didn't pulse like that before." Gabriel held up a hand, letting his palm dance and stop. "That sounds... new."

His mom went over to a door not far from the tank, where a window separated them from a larger section of the lab with tables and computer monitors. Mom rapped on the glass and pressed a call button next to the door. "Sharmila?"

A woman inside the lab came on the line. "Doctor?"

"Are we ready to look at the tissue sample?"

"Just about." Gabriel's mom left them for a moment as

the rest remained with his dad at the window. Gabriel tapped on the glass. The microphone hanging nearby picked up the vibrations as a sharp tone, which he heard in his earpiece. The enormous Lodger swiveled in place, finally looking toward the glass.

The creature flexed its tentacles and whined. Gabriel thumped the glass with his fingers.

This time the creature did something new—its tentacles spun rapidly. Some unknown set of muscles moved and allowed it to send out a different, deeper whine, like the purr of a cat but musical—a sea-thrumming, he thought.

"Try that again," Dad said.

Gabriel tapped the glass again, and it answered.

"Huh," Peter said. His eyes narrowed as though he was thinking through something.

"What is it?" Gabriel asked.

Peter shrugged. "I don't know yet. Try that again."

A third time tapping and the creature was still. *I guess it's bored now,* Gabriel thought. As though it had tried to communicate with them and its effort had failed, and now it had written them off. The way you might startle at first at a hat rack that looks like a person in the dark, but after a while, you blow it off because it's just a hat rack. But what if it were a person after all?

Gabriel's mom stuck her head out of the lab door—another flash of warmth, a faint memory of seeing her calling him into a lecture when he was too small to even have a clear memory—and said, "Okay. Care to see where your friend is from?" She added with a pleasant shrug, "If possible?"

Gabriel felt a thrill of expectation. They had taken a couple of tiny samples of tissue from the creature while loading it into the tank, and Sharmila Kassam, the head of genetic studies at the lab, had hurried it away in small sample jar.

He followed the others into the lab.

The lab was circular, occupying the bottom floor of a dome dedicated to biological studies. The walls curved, jutting every so often with mechanical arms holding lights, lasers, cutting tools, and other instruments. Soft lamps in recesses around the room gave off a bright glow. There were no portholes out. As the door hissed closed, Gabriel heard locks inside clamping down. This room was built to be isolated if necessary, sanitized with strong corrosives or, if *really* necessary, far more permanent solutions.

They joined Dr. Kassam next to a microscope at a table near the center of the room. She wore a white cap over her hair, which flowed in a neat tail down her back.

Gabriel had known Sharmila Kassam, one of the five non-family humans who lived at Nemolab, since he was three years old. He was originally told that she had come to learn from them, the way the Nobel scientist had. But eventually he learned there was more. Sharmila had been the only survivor of a terrorist attack on a science ship where her parents had worked. A genius, she had already been doing doctorate-level work at seventeen years old. She had lost both her parents and their experiments—on nonnuclear deep-sea engines—in one day. Some crazy enemies of the Nemos had been behind the attack. Apparently Mom and Dad had rescued her themselves. He had never gotten the whole story, but as the years went by, he suspected it had been harder than it sounded.

But still the story—even as far as he knew it—stuck with him. His parents rarely left the lab or approached other ships or land—and yet sometime back then they'd had their own wild lives and adventures. It was impossible for him to picture.

His mom approached the eyepiece of the microscope, peered into it for a moment, and then said, "Hmm. Let's project this." She hit a button beside the microscope, and a three-foot-wide screen on the wall lit up.

Onscreen, they saw a magnified world of moving matter, which Gabriel expected. He saw tiny masses teeming with what looked like hairs up and down their bodies as they danced in the saline solution that held the sample. In biology, both at the lab and in his time at school in Santa Marta, he'd seen a few such samples, and nothing here jumped out at him.

His mom took a pen out of her hair and pointed at the screen. "This is a scraping from one of the tentacles, from the sort of frond at the end where it gets wide. In every respect I would say what we are looking at is definitely crustacean. I'm seeing the usual mucus, proteins, fats. Now can we look at the second specimen?"

Dr. Kassam moved a second glass plate into place under the microscope, and the screen changed.

Mom said, "This is a scraping from those little... what you called bulbs."

"You're lucky it didn't burn you."

"I think they only burn when they want to," Mom said. "But look at this tissue."

She indicated squarish structures, blocks up and down the surface of the specimen. "You know what that is? That's white sulfuric crystal. Embedded in the skin. Only here, though."

Misty peered at it. "Crystal?"

"Why would they look like crystal?" asked Peter.

"Because they *are* crystal." Gabriel's dad moved closer to the screen and put his hands in the pockets of his white smock.

Gabriel looked back at the rest. "They use these— bulbs—to burn out the insides of the machines they take over. But they're not actually part of the Lodgers. They're more like..."

"Like snails on a plant," Dad said. "The bulbs on the tentacle fronds are different creatures entirely."

17

THEY WERE DUE for dinner, but there was something Gabriel wanted to take care of first: the engines. Peter was interested in spending some more time at the Lodger window, so Gabriel and Misty headed back to the access tube and the *Obscure*. Along the way they stopped at a supply room, and the lights came on as they entered.

"What are we looking for?" Misty asked, scanning shelves and shelves of engine parts, rivets, and even a few disassembled pincer torpedoes.

Gabriel found it: a large black cylinder about the size of a watermelon, with tubes and wires on either end. "This." He held it up with both hands. "It's an engine filter for the *Nebula*."

"Will that keep us from fouling up in the Garbage Patch?"

Gabriel nodded. "It should. We just gotta fit it to the *Obscure*."

∼∼⌒

Inside the engine room, as Misty crouched and unscrewed the bolts on the old filter, she changed the subject back to the Lodgers. "Symbiotic," she said. "The Lodgers are in a symbiotic relationship."

"Yeah." Gabriel was on the floor again, unscrewing another connector. He actually loved being under the engine. "Like the eels that hang around whales."

"You ready for this to come loose?"

"Yeah, drop it." He looked up as she let the end of the old filter fall out of place, and together they maneuvered it to the floor. He took one end of the new filter, and she started fastening the other end.

"Symbiotic relationships are so strange."

"Why's that?" Gabriel screwed the bolts into place.

"I mean—what do we do, as a species?" She fastened her end. "We grow to be our best selves. Right? Humans get smarter. Birds get faster. Worms get to break in two and form another worm. But to decide my best self is a self with . . . another self?"

Gabriel was satisfied with the connection and slid out, sitting up. "That sounds deep."

"I'm sorry. I'm just loving the mystery." She patted the connection of the filter and sat down.

He was glad she was loving it. But once again it made him remember what she'd said about her parents. "You know, I was thinking. I could have my parents call yours. If they can call Mr. Zinoman, they can call your folks."

Misty shook her head. "No . . . my folks said yes. Calling them in a panic wouldn't help. I'm where I said I'd be. Sort of."

Gabriel sighed in relief. Then he shrugged. "Finish the trip. Then when we're home, if you're out, you're out." *Please don't be out.*

"What I want to finish is helping that thing in the dome." She pointed over her shoulder, through the wall of the engine room. "That's it."

"Gabriel?" His dad's voice came over the intercom. "If you have time before dinner, there's something I'd love to show you guys."

Gabriel looked at Misty and shrugged.

They met up with Peter and Nerissa, who had each gotten the same invitation, and found Gabriel's dad at the entrance to a large, rectangular room with a curved roof. It was one of the few rooms exposed to the outside that wasn't a dome shape, and the curve of the ceiling made strange refractions of the seaweed and fish that floated by. The tile floor was polished volcanic rock and reflected them perfectly as they walked along.

But the main thing about the room was the models. *What in the world?*

There were eight short columns in the center of the room, and each one held a perfect scale model of a submarine.

"Whoa." Peter stopped short.

Gabriel's dad smiled. "Yeah. I've had a little time on my hands lately and I thought—well, I know Gabriel used to like to look at pictures of the old ships. I figured I could do better. Take a look! This one..."

"Dad, I'm not sure we have time..." Nerissa sounded more hesitant talking to him, her voice a little higher.

"I figured. Gabriel has brought his crew," Dad said. "And it matters to understand where we're coming from. Come on, I'll bet you'll get something out of it, too."

Gabriel was lost for a moment looking at the ships and heard his throat catch as he replied, "Yeah. Give us the tour."

"By all means," Nerissa mumbled.

Dad arranged himself behind the models and stretched his hands wide toward the two subs that Gabriel's friends would be familiar with. "This is the fleet. Not even the whole fleet, I guess, but most of it. You know the *Obscure*, and of course, this big thing is the *Nebula*." He pointed to the sleek black sub with its pointed nose and a ship three times larger perched on a column.

He indicated the other subs, some of them short and

squat, some long, some with strange up-and-down arrangements instead of "lying down" horizontally. But all had the same eye for the sea, the fins and the seashell inlays, the sense of belonging in the deep.

"Toward the back are the ones that came earlier. *Arronax*, named after the man who traveled with our ancestor. That one saved President Eisenhower's life once. Decommissioned in 1965. Before that, *Prince Dakkar*, which ferried the crown jewels of England to Japan and back in a pretty strange gambit that would be way too difficult to explain."

"Wait, excuse me?" Peter asked. "Why?"

"Seriously, we don't have time for that." Nerissa shook her head.

"*Prince Dakkar* was . . . well, let's say *lost*, but it's complicated. Before that, here's *Paravar*, the first to explore the Mariana Trench. It was taken by pirates and destroyed. *Eye of Providence*, used for listening to ships, mainly. Decommissioned in the 1920s. That was during the quiet period after Captain Nemo ended his reign of . . . I guess his reign of terror. That brings us to the *Nautilus*."

The tip of the pyramid shape, farthest from Gabriel's dad and closest to the rest, was a final submarine, the earliest. A little bigger than the *Obscure* but slower, with a battering nose like the *Nebula* but sharpened with a corkscrew point. "The *Nautilus*, the ship of Captain Nemo."

Gabriel's dad was silent for a moment as he stared at it, and Misty spoke. "What happened to the *Nautilus*?"

Gabriel's dad looked up. "You can get closer—take a look at it. It's beautiful. The *Nautilus* was damaged in a storm—the legendary 'maelstrom.' Captain Nemo kept it on the island at the yard where we build the ships while he worked his repairs."

"That location is secret," Nerissa added.

"Yeah. But it did sail again, and then it was lost during a mission in the Pacific."

"Where in the Pacific?" Misty asked.

"We don't know." Gabriel's dad shrugged. "Could be anywhere from Mexico to Japan. But by that time Captain Nemo was very old. And the family had begun its work already. And so it was . . . lost."

"So . . . every ship you built here is gone. Almost." Peter put his hands in his pockets. As though it was sinking in what a special place he was inhabiting. "The *Obscure* and the *Nebula* are the last of the Nemotech subs."

"Not the last." Gabriel's dad went to the door and beckoned them. "We like to think of them as a new beginning. Come on. Dinner."

18

FOR THE FIRST time in nearly a year, Gabriel had dinner at Nemolab, and it was glorious. At least to him. For once, the dining hall, which occupied its own dome to the side of the main one, was almost crowded. One long table held Gabriel, his parents, Peter, Misty, and the five trusted guests of Nemolab who helped run the different sections. Plus two more: Nerissa had invited her executive officer, Jaideep, to represent her crew (the rest of the three hundred remained aboard the *Nebula*, presumably doing whatever they usually did in the evening). Dad served up a seaweed-based lasagna that even Peter loved. Behind them, strange fish swam around the dome, zooming past in swirls of color and speckled schools.

Mom was more talkative than he had ever seen and

seemed determined to embarrass him, loudly entertaining everyone with stories of Gabriel and Nerissa when they were smaller. "When Gabriel was eight, they watched this thing about a singer. You know, he wants to make it big as a singer with a band."

"That could be anything," Peter said.

"He had a maroon motorcycle," Mom said. "*Il Pleut Mauve*?"

"*Purple Rain*," Nerissa and Gabriel answered.

"That movie's like a hundred years old."

"Oh, come on," Gabriel said. "I lived on the bottom of the ocean; for me that was a great movie. First thing I did when I got to California was look to see if Morris Day and the Time were still around." That was the hilarious band in *Purple Rain*.

"Were they?" Dad asked.

"Not as much as you might think." Gabriel laughed.

"You should have seen the clothes Gabriel demanded that year," Mom went on. "An eight-year-old boy in puffy-sleeved blouses."

"You make blouses?" Misty rested her chin on her hand, a forkful of lasagna dangling.

"Do you have pictures?" Peter asked.

"Oh, you bet," said Nerissa.

She laughed, and Jaideep added, "We have *all* of them on the *Nebula* database."

Mom patted Nerissa's hand, her eyes crinkling.

"So is that what it was like?" Misty asked. "Just the four of you, studying, watching movies?"

"Movies were strictly regulated," Dad said. "But Dr. Nemo had a soft spot for Prince from her days topside." He meant Gabriel's mom.

"But weren't you . . . lonely?" Misty pressed on.

Gabriel's parents looked at each other uncomfortably, and his dad waved a hand. He pointed a knife at a cloud of brilliantly colored jellyfish that spun and swarmed up along the dome. "You can't be lonely. Not with that out there."

"That's why the *experiment*," Mom said. "We raised Gabriel and Nerissa to be a part of the Nemo vision, to be one with the sea. But after a while it was time to see if Gabriel could bring that vision to the land."

"Just Gabriel?"

"Oh, I was gone by then," Nerissa said.

Mom smiled, or tried to. "You, too. We would have done the same with you."

"Would you?" Nerissa dabbed her mouth with a golden napkin embroidered with an *N*. "Because what I remember is that you didn't want us out there. Not in the dirty world. Except you're willing to send *him* to land with *no guidance*. Oh, except you set him up with a *lawyer*."

"Nerissa." Gabriel lowered his voice as if he could mentally force her to do the same.

"No, if they want me to shut up they're totally capable of saying it, Gabriel."

"Was there bread?" Peter asked, searching the table. "I could have sworn there was bread."

"We were getting reports, daily reports, that there were pirates who had ships like ours, hiring out their services to anyone who would pay, and what were they doing? Using technology stolen from *us* in the service of navies, of whalers, of smugglers. And what did we do? *Nothing.*"

Gabriel blanched and tried to explain. "We were working on the *Nebula*."

"Which I had to *steal* to get any good out of it," Nerissa snarled. Peter reached across her to get at a basket of sea-cucumber bread, and Nerissa picked it up and slammed it down in front of him.

"Even we never accused you of that." Mom looked down, hurt showing on her face. "What's ours is yours."

"And isn't *that* convenient? So you can keep your hands clean in this hermetically sealed...*Shangri-la.*"

"Nerissa!" Dad looked appalled. "*Stop.*"

Gabriel felt bad for him. His dad was...complicated. He represented a family known for raining terror on the seas, and he'd worked to change that, but it was as if the adventurous Nemo spirit had a dark half that seeped through. Had that infected Nerissa? Or was she just rebelling against their ideas the way anybody might, just wanting to tick off her parents? But he could see on his dad's face that it was killing him that there wasn't a thing he could do about it. Gabriel wanted to shout and come to his parents' defense

181

even though part of him was with Nerissa. They didn't really take the world seriously, not the way Nerissa did.

And this was supposed to be a *nice* dinner.

Nerissa looked like she was about to hurl her plate before she stiffened her shoulders. "I have some studying to do." She rose and left her napkin on the plate, then strode out.

Jaideep excused himself and headed for whatever room they'd assigned him in the dormitory.

The spell was broken and everyone separated. "I want to check out the Lodger some more," Gabriel said. "Misty and Peter, you want to . . . ?"

They nodded silently and followed him. Gabriel kissed his mom on the cheek, feeling the warmth of her skin against his lips. He walked quickly, his own cheeks burning. *Nerissa, why do you have to ruin everything?*

As the crew of the *Obscure* exited into the corridor, Peter slapped Gabriel on the shoulder. "Wow."

"What?" Gabriel asked, staring at his boots as he walked. The corridor was all Nemoglass, the whole sea beyond, but he couldn't draw any comfort from it.

Peter laughed. "It *is* a normal family."

19

THEY STOPPED AT the window before the Lodger's dome. Gabriel felt his cheeks still burning with embarrassment.

Peter saw how uncomfortable he was and said, "Check this out." He switched on the microphone next to the one-way mirror. The Lodger on the other side swam around the space of the holding dome. Peter started to rap on the mirror when Misty interrupted him.

"Hey." She tilted her head toward Gabriel as they stood next to the glass. "You okay?"

"He's okay," Peter said. "This is family stuff."

"Peter, aren't you, like, an only child?"

"Ouch."

"I'm sorry," Misty said to Peter. Then to Gabriel, "You, too."

"It's not my problem." Gabriel shook his head. "Nerissa is who she is." That wasn't enough, but it was as much as he could bring himself to say.

"Okay," Peter said. "I've been thinking about this. Now watch." He thumped the glass rapidly, a series of steady bumps.

The Lodger shifted, the whale-sized body twisting, its crawfish head pointed away from them.

He did it again. Now the creature seemed to look up, the head turning toward them. Something inside it responded, a long purr of multiple beats echoing in the water.

Misty listened. "Bumps. Like the drumming of the whales."

"Yeah. You do the pattern like they make; they make it back," Peter said. "Or at least I was hoping they would. And they did!"

"Huh," Gabriel said. "So if we wanted to send a series of bumps, tones like this, what would you use?"

Peter nodded. "Like how much, how many?"

"Like a lot, steady and regular."

Peter considered it. "We have the sonar pings. Yeah!" he said excitedly. "You could use the sonar array."

"So you could send a whole *bunch*." Misty nodded. "Bump bump bump. But it would sound like sonar."

"Yeah." Peter agreed. "But we could lower the frequency. Then the bumps would sound…deeper."

The creature sent out a series of whining bumps.

"Like that?" Gabriel motioned toward the window.

"Sure." Peter was nodding. "And you know what? I'll bet I can make it portable."

~~~

Gabriel ran down a shimmering white corridor to the private rooms of the Nemo family, yelling as he went. He knocked on his parents' door and then raced across the hall to Nerissa's room, yelling the universal code for *everyone get out here*. "Hey! Hey! Mom, Dad, Nerissa! Hey! Up every soul!"

He heard pounding footsteps, and Nerissa ripped her door open. She was wearing black pajamas. "What is it?"

"I want you to see something."

Down the hall, his mom and dad were looking out of their room in matching silver robes that made them look like aliens in an old movie. "What?"

Nerissa looked annoyed. "You said 'Up every soul.'"

"Well, yeah. This is amazing."

"You only use that when people are *dying*," Nerissa called, but he was already running back toward the lab.

"Well, you will *die* when you see it."

When his parents and Nerissa joined them back at the one-way mirror, Gabriel was standing before a table he and his friends had set up. Next to a bunch of tools they had a junction box with a few knobs. "You have the batteries charged?"

"Yep," Peter answered.

"Hi, guys," Gabriel said brightly as the rest came in from the corridor.

Nerissa frowned. "This had better be good."

Misty turned to them all. "One of the questions we've been asking is how the Lodgers communicate. With one another. Because we know they guard one another and co-ordinate themselves."

"That doesn't necessarily mean they communicate," Nerissa countered. "Beavers build dams, but it's largely instinct. They're not going out and drawing up blueprints. Salmon all swim upstream, but they're not mapping it out on Google beforehand."

"But they're not beavers," Misty insisted. "They *do* communicate. There's variety. There's that whining scream we heard when they yelled at us. But otherwise they send out what I'd call signals. Like..."

"Like whales," Gabriel continued. "But maybe smarter. I want you to see what we've come up with."

He bounced excitedly as he stood before the holding tank. The creature within hung in the water as if waiting while he spoke. "We thought the thrumming sound it made with its tentacles and body sounded like some effort at communication. It even moved excitedly when I tapped on the glass in response. So Peter"—he rubbed the back of his friend's head, making the hair all stand up—"the *genius*, rigged up *this*."

Peter showed them a box. It had an antenna on the end and a small dish that made it look something like an alarm clock. There was a button in the center and a pair of sliders on either side. "This is crude…but it works."

"What does it do?" Nerissa reached out, but Peter held it back.

"Ah, let me *show* you." Peter pressed the button as he held the box near the glass. At first it was hard to hear, but then he moved a slider and they heard it more clearly—a rhythmic thrumming emanated from the dish toward the glass, *fwow-wow-wow-wow-wow-wow*.

The creature perked up, turning toward the sound. It trilled in the water, its tentacles vibrating and answering the hum. Peter turned the box, pointing it toward the other end of the tank, and pressed again, emitting a higher-pitched *fwow-wow-wow-wow-wow-wow*.

The creature moved in the water, the whole enormous body sailing toward the end he was pointing at.

"Oh, wow." Gabriel's mom clasped her hands. "You can direct it."

"Yes. Meet the Crabsiren," Peter said.

"Crabsiren?" Nerissa asked.

"Just what we're calling it for now," Gabriel said. Misty subtly shook her head because she hated the name. Everyone was a critic.

"Crabsiren is go!" Peter pressed the button, and the Lodger slowly swam in the direction he pointed. He turned up the volume, pointing at the top of the tank. The Lodger rose steadily, echoing the Crabsiren's volume. The thrumming coming over the speakers intensified. Peter looked back to the rest. "And this is just the beginning. There's no telling what we might be able to work out in time."

Misty went on, "What does the rhythm mean, for instance? Maybe we can develop a whole vocabulary."

Nerissa crossed her arms. For once, she looked impressed. "You guys. This is good. We're learning a lot."

The creature swept a tentacle frond by the window, and Gabriel's dad cleared his throat. "I wanted to say, there's something else. Something Nerissa reminded me of when she called us a *Shangri-la*. See, that was a famous place of exotic creatures and plants."

"Dad..."

"Save it," their dad said. He looked out at the beast in the dome. "The Lodgers are two creatures, we said. Right? The crustacean, hermit-crab kind of creature, and these wormlike appendages that let them burn through metal. When we looked at the samples we saw that they were partially crystallized. There was something familiar about it that I had to think about."

"And?" Looking at his dad, Gabriel remembered hundreds of moments just like this, standing next to Nerissa under a dome while his father lectured them about marine biology.

"We have exotic places down here, too. I've only ever seen biology like that in one spot." His dad turned around. "The Black Smokers."

20

GABRIEL TRIED TO keep up with Nerissa's insistent stride as they walked rapidly through white corridors toward the equipment they'd need. Misty matched him step for step, Peter close behind.

"The *Obscure*'s engines are still being looked at, your little side trip notwithstanding," Nerissa said. "And anyway, you wouldn't have the room. We're going to take the *Nebula*. You." Nerissa stopped, pointing at Peter.

Peter practically gulped. "Me?"

"You're the helm on the *Obscure*?"

"Yes, for nearly six months."

"Good, we'll need another driver." They, reached a large rectangular hatch the size of a garage door, and Nerissa put her palm on a Nemotech icon beside the door.

Peter whispered at Gabriel as the door slid open. "To drive *what?*"

"To drive *that*."

Beyond the door was a massive hangar where Gabriel could see rows upon rows of equipment and vehicles—light trucks, forklifts, a few small subs under construction, even a pair of helicopters that could be carried up to the surface to whisk critically injured personnel off to some mainland or another.

Gabriel felt a swell of pride looking at the hangar. Weird recluses or not, the Nemos had some cool toys.

Nerissa was pointing at a vehicle about fifty feet away to the left.

"This is a Nemotech rover." The vehicle was roughly the size of a minibus, with heavy armor and extended axles holding massive tires with deep scallops in the tread. The one Nerissa hurried to now was the same deep green as Gabriel's dive suit, but parked near it were five more, each in an equally dark but different color. She beckoned Peter closer. "Climb up on the wheel well and look in."

Peter did so while Gabriel and the rest crowded around. Inside, they could see multiple seats that stopped at a partition labeled AIR LOCK.

In the driver's seat were a joystick and a tablet display, currently dark.

"How does it...?"

"It drives like a sub—one of ours, anyway."

"The idea was that if you could learn the controls of a Nemotech sub, you could drive any of the other vehicles," Gabriel offered, though he sensed that Nerissa didn't want his interruption. Still. He had helped put these things together, and anyway, she'd left *before* he did—how did she know they hadn't completely changed everything while she was gone? She was lucky her palm print still worked the doors.

Misty raised an eyebrow. *Let her do her thing.*

"Get in." Nerissa pulled a lever and the door opened up. Peter stared at it.

"I've never driven this before."

"Yeah, but you know how. And there's no time like the present. And anyway, we need someone to drive it to the *Nebula.*"

"Is it..." He touched the ceiling inside, which was festooned with countless buttons and switches. But his hand went to the rivets along the thick windows. "Watertight?"

"Well, it could function as a sub if the air lock were compromised. If that happens"—Nerissa leaned in, pointing at a panel over the driver's seat—"there's a mask in there. And a high-pressure suit to get into. Uh, and quickly, because the pressure down here will kill you, so you'll have about ninety seconds after water starts coming in to..."

"Hang on!" Peter waved his hands. "Wait just a minute. Now you're talking about the ocean floor. As in outside the sub and crawling on the bottom like a crab."

Gabriel frowned. He didn't want to embarrass Peter, but this had to be said. "We have a deal. Peter doesn't get wet."

"He doesn't get *wet*?" Nerissa's lip curled.

Gabriel nodded. Misty folded her arms. "That's the deal."

"It..." Peter wobbled his head. "Yeah, that's the deal."

"Why can't *your* helmsman do it?" Gabriel offered.

"I need him for the *Nebula*."

"Just..." Gabriel waved a hand. "What does Peter need to do?"

Nerissa pinched the bridge of her nose for a second. "Okay. Listen. Peter. You won't get wet. I've taken this thing out to four miles down. The external skin has never leaked. The air lock is the only concern, so watch the integrity gauge and make sure she stays cool enough. In the end, it's the same job."

"Are you sure?"

"I lead a crew of three hundred souls." Nerissa put her hand on Peter's shoulder as he looked up at her. "And I don't betray their trust."

"Me, either," Gabriel added. "It's the same job."

Peter paused, then nodded. "You owe me big time."

"Sure do." Gabriel clapped Peter on the shoulder.

"Are you ready to see the suits?" came Gabriel's dad's voice from the entry to the hangar. They turned around to see he'd changed into a deep-green jumpsuit. He was walking across the hangar to an area in the back enclosed in white metal walls.

"What kind of suits?" Misty asked as they all ran after him.

He opened the door, and they entered a room that Gabriel had not been inside for years. There were lockers along one wall and all manner of diving apparatus stored on shelves, with multiple suits hanging from metal arms.

"Now." Dad pressed a button and a rod extended with a silvery suit hanging off it. He ran a hand along it. "We designed this Nemosuit for extreme environments. It can handle ocean-floor depths and even space."

"*Space?*" Peter asked.

"Well, that was what they wanted."

"Who's they?" Misty asked.

"Doesn't matter," Nerissa mumbled.

"Oh, come on." This was one of Gabriel's favorite things about the family. "Mom and Dad design all kinds of stuff for *all* kinds of people. I'm talking government, NASA, NOAA, navy, private guys like SpaceX, weird guys like HEXEN and the Polidorium, universities…"

"Yeah, anyway." Dad nodded. "Space."

The chest of the suit, which shimmered blue and green, was armored and sectioned to allow for movement. "This is hard stuff." He rapped the chest plate. "I wouldn't walk into a torpedo with it, but…" He shrugged. "Come on, feel."

Misty went up and ran her hands along the limbs. "There's stuff in the sleeves ... and the knees."

Gabriel's dad grinned. "Yeah. Exoskeleton. Processor in the helmet gives you assisted walking."

"Good for the moon?" asked Peter.

"Don't answer that," Nerissa said. "So now that you've seen them, grab two. We have a sub to catch."

21

GABRIEL FOUND HIMSELF at a loss for what to do on Nerissa's bridge. It was bigger than the *Obscure*'s bridge, with twice the stations and room to breathe, but all the stations were manned and for once he was just ballast, weight to be carried. Nerissa stayed at her spot in front of the view screen, and Gabriel watched with her for a while. He looked back at the crewmen working away at their stations. Jaideep was at a nearby console, and Gabriel dropped his voice. "What are you carrying on this ship? I mean, if we need to defend ourselves?"

"A heck of a battering ram." Nerissa tilted her head toward the nose of the ship.

"Torpedoes?"

She nodded. "Yeah, those, too."

"Pincers?"

"Some."

Gabriel stuck his hands in his pockets. "Would you do me a favor and use those? If there's trouble?"

Now she turned and looked at him. "What do you mean, if there's trouble?"

"I mean it would go a long way, with anyone, if we didn't use explosives. Knock 'em out, but for heaven's sake we should try not to . . . you know, murder anyone."

She bit her lip. "Gabriel, what do you think you're doing right now?"

"I'm just—"

"This is my ship." Nerissa turned back to the screen. "We use whatever I say we use."

He tried to speak several times more in the span of a few minutes. He wanted to change the subject, to ask her what else she'd been doing for the past year, but finally he realized she wasn't having it and gave up. He went into the study where Peter and Misty were.

Peter was at the edge of a loveseat, bent forward and intently studying a tablet with schematics of the rover. Misty was at the table with a sketchpad and pencil, working at what Gabriel thought was a picture of the Lodger from the tank. The one that had first been inside a biplane.

Misty put down her pencil. "What's going on out there?"

Gabriel shrugged and sat. "I was getting in the way."

"How much longer is it?"

"About an hour."

Peter put down the tablet. "I can't look at this anymore. Do you think there's a galley? This thing's gotta have a kitchen."

Gabriel pointed. "Through that hatch, through three more hatches, up two. Just aft of center."

"Anyone want anything?"

Misty stretched. "Soda. Something with caffeine. Extra points if it's not the Nemo brand."

"No one likes my soda," Gabriel moaned.

"Eh, the seaweed lasagna was great, but the soda needs work," Misty said.

"Done." Peter disappeared through the hatch.

Misty looked out the window at the ocean. "Was it true, the thing you said to Nerissa, that your mom and dad knew you were bringing a crew?"

Gabriel nodded. "Yeah, it's true that I had Zinoman tell them that if they had a problem with it they should speak up."

She put her hands on the table. "You get it, right?"

"Get what?"

"The thing is, what Nerissa does, what you do, it means making all these decisions. We talked about what I thought about lying."

"I know, I know," Gabriel said.

"Nerissa just wants to make sure you're *ready*. I mean, forget what I feel bad about. You risk so much, and you think you know what you're doing, but you can't know everything. You can't. I think she wants you to do good, and she doesn't want to see you suffer any more than you have to. But to her that means you shouldn't be saddled with people you have to be in charge of."

Gabriel looked at the table. Everything Misty said was true. "It's too late *now*."

"But that's not it. You're not your sister. Nerissa wears her isolation like a badge. You're different," she said. "We're not just your crew. We're your friends. And that means there's nothing here you're going to have to go through alone."

An hour later and a hundred and fifty miles from the location of Nemolab, Gabriel and Misty stepped out of the air lock, lumbering down the roughly textured hatch at the back of the rover.

"Everyone copy?" Gabriel spoke into the microphone at the edge of his helmet, his boot landing in soft earth at the bottom of the ocean.

Beside him, Misty held up a thickly gloved thumb. "Copy." Her face was lit all around by tiny lights inside a large green helmet that curved like a conch shell at the back. Like Gabriel, she looked like some kind of robot, with her armored chest and mechanically assisted limbs.

The hatch silently closed behind them as Peter sounded off. "Copy."

"Copy," came Nerissa's voice from the *Nebula*, a massive dark obstruction hanging above them, stationary in the water. "We've got you on camera, and your systems in the rover look normal."

"Thanks," Peter answered. "So far I've only driven this thing about sixty yards, but she handles okay."

A slight chuckle. "You dry?"

"As a bone, Captain Nemo."

"Copy that. Now, there are thermal pockets all along the floor here, guys, so be ready to move if..."

"If what?" Gabriel asked.

"You know, if it opens up."

"The *floor*?"

Nerissa came back, "Yeah, if the floor opens up and... lava comes out."

Gabriel shook his head. "Copy. We'll collect the samples and hopefully, you know, that won't happen."

Gabriel and Misty turned away from the back of the rover and faced their objective. Gabriel switched on a lamp on his shoulder, and it cast a wide, bright beam through the water, lighting the way.

"It's amazing," Misty whispered through the mic.

"Yes, it is." About a football field away, a cluster of tall, natural columns of earth and coral-like structures thrust up. Out of stovepipelike mouths in each, plumes of dark smoke poured into the ocean. The Black Smokers were one of the most mysterious phenomena of the sea, only discovered in the last fifty years. Some were short, and some reached twenty feet high with masses of something that looked like crystal clustered around.

"I thought thermal vents were just seams in the ground."

"Well, sort of." Gabriel walked steadily, rotors in his knees sounding and making it easier to take long strides. Clouds of sea dust sifted around his legs, and he watched white crabs that would never see the sun scamper away. "But the Black Smokers are more than just heat rising from the center of the earth. They react with the local flora, causing the columns you see and forming a strange habitat."

"You're lecturing again." He could see Misty's smile through the helmet.

"Well, we did say this was an educational tour." He flexed his arms. They were slightly cool, even though he knew the temperature in the water here had to be near boiling. The suits were working perfectly. Then it started to warm up fast.

After about five minutes of walking they came to some smaller smokers, a cluster about Gabriel's height. He stood at a distance, watching the smoke. "You starting to feel it?"

"Yeah, it's hot." Crabs skittered around, and small creatures that looked like crawdads moved backward around the smoke. Every creature had long antennae that picked and poked at the air. "What are the red-and-white plumes?" She pointed to masses of long, strawlike structures about half an inch wide that curved around the top of the smokers.

"Those are tube worms," Gabriel said. "These kind only grow here, getting nutrients from the smoke and the matter that is burned up in the heat. They grow and they grow, and they'll remain in place for hundreds of years."

Misty pulled a sample collector jar out of a pouch at her waist. She popped it open, and the lid acted as a spoon as she cautiously approached the white crystals. "I'll get a bit of the vegetation."

"Sure, leave me to chase a crab around the place." The heat grew more noticeable as they came closer. "Move fast and low."

Gabriel saw a crab moving sideways around the base of the smoker and crouched. He had collected crabs before. He put his hand down, blocking the tiny white creature's path, and it immediately darted in the opposite direction. It smacked into the rim of his jar and bounced away. Okay, so he was out of practice.

He glanced over to see Misty, who had dropped to her knees to scoop some crystals off the side of the smoker. A halo of red-and-white worms surrounded her helmeted head, clinging to the side of the column.

Gabriel found another crab and performed the same

maneuver as before, and this time the crab darted right into the jar, and he closed it with a satisfying *click.*

"I've got my sample." Misty stood up, backing away as she put the jar in her pouch. "Let's go."

Gabriel still crouched in the silt when the worms near Misty's head fluttered and—they couldn't move, could they? But they *were!* "Misty, watch out!"

She looked sideways as a handful of foot-long white worms broke free from the column and wriggled through the air, landing on her shoulders. One of them landed on her helmet, clapping itself along her faceplate. "What the . . . ?" She brushed at it, but it held there as she brushed at it again, stepping away as if to escape.

Gabriel ran, or tried to run, to her side, the rotors helping him to a slow plod. "That's amazing. I've never heard of them doing that." He reached out with his glove and grabbed one of the tube worms on her shoulder. It flexed under his fingers like a piece of thick white pasta, and then it curled up and latched onto his fingers.

"I've picked one up."

"What are you seeing?" Nerissa asked in his ear.

"Tube worms, but they're being . . . aggressive."

"Get out of there."

"They don't bite."

"Gabriel, crazy things happen. Move."

A cloud of the creatures let loose from the column and undulated through the water, landing on his shoulders.

"Come on." He started to move back. "We've got scrapers in the rover, we can peel them off…"

And then he heard a hiss. Water was evaporating on his glove as the creature there glowed, moving around his palm and wrist. For a brief moment he saw its underbelly as it moved. A long, thin seam had opened up along the side of the worm, and inside, brightly burning matter made water molecules explode. It clamped on his hand and started to burn.

"Argh." Misty swiped at her shoulder. "This thing is burning me."

"Yeah, it's got my hand… They're burning through the suits."

They started to move as quickly as they could, making long jumping strides along the ocean floor. The things were burning through the way the bulbs of the Lodgers did. No: These *were* the bulbs.

Misty yelped, and he looked over to see that there was vapor coming off her faceplate as the worm worked its way along the glass. A red glow shone on her face from the underside of the worm.

He didn't hear but saw a crack form in her faceplate. "Stop." He took her by the arm.

"We have to go—"

"We won't get anywhere if they melt through our faceplates," he said urgently. That would cause water to rush in and drown them instantly. The same if the worms burned through their suits. They were just asking to let the water in if they didn't get rid of these things.

The worm at his hand was making his fingers numb with heat, and he grabbed it with his other hand, ripping it away and hoping it wouldn't take a chunk of his glove with it. He immediately brought it up in an arc, still burning. Gabriel slapped it against the worm on Misty's faceplate, and water exploded all around them. The worm on her helmet tore itself away, twisting into the darkness.

"Now run." The burns were all over his suit now—he could feel them on his shoulder, back, and legs.

As they came within yards of the back of the rover, a bright seam opened up in the floor about ten yards in front of it. "Heat!" Peter shouted. The ground moved beneath them and made the rover shake as a boiling wave of heat blew against the vehicle. "Hurry up, Captain."

"Rover, we are reading massive heat surges in your suppressors," Nerissa's voice came on the mic. "Your engines won't take that for too long. You need to move off so we can collect you."

"He needs to collect *us* first." Gabriel ripped a worm from his knee. He squeezed it and then tore his fingers away from it as it blazed like a torch and fled. "Open hatch."

"I'm opening the door." The rear door of the rover started to come down, and Gabriel and Misty climbed onto it before it was even all the way open, tumbling through water into the air lock.

"Close it, close it." Gabriel landed on his shoulder on the floor and came to his knees. "We're clear."

The hatch closed and Peter started to drive, the big wheels outside the portholes kicking up a storm of sea dust.

Misty gasped as a worm at her hip sizzled, and he saw the fabric of her suit bubble. "Scrapers."

"We need tools," Gabriel called to Peter. "The tools in the back of the cockpit. Blow out the air lock, double-time."

"Blowing the air lock," Peter said.

There was a moment of silence and then... nothing. The vents in the back should have opened to pump water out, but nothing was happening.

"Peter?" A worm at Gabriel's chest started to burn through and he could feel the heat at his sternum, heat that undulated with thousands of the worm's tiny movements.

"Uh, air lock is malfunctioning." Peter's voice was agitated. "I think the controls have been damaged by the heat."

A worm flared at his other knee and Gabriel cried out in pain, dropping, scraping at it with his fingers. "Look for a manual override."

"I'm trying. All the auxiliary functions are offline."

"We are sending down cables to grab the rover," Nerissa said.

Gabriel fought to find the worms as Misty writhed next to him in her own battle. He saw one behind her neck and grabbed it. "Here, can you get this one?" He wriggled his head at the back of his shoulder and she grabbed it, dropping it into the water. In his earpiece, Nerissa was saying that mechanical cables were coming down to grab the rods at the top of the rover and haul it up to the *Nebula*'s own dive room, but—

"There isn't time," Gabriel insisted. "We're trapped in the air lock, and these things are going to burn through our suits."

He managed to get the worm free from his knee and saw that a piece of fabric came with it. The inside lining was still there but if that ruptured, water would rush all the way up to his helmet. And he would drown, right here in the back of this vehicle.

The worm in his hand bounced back and landed on his face, burning. The helmet started to bubble as red flame filled his eyes. *What are you?*

A crack sounded in his ear as the glass began to rupture in front of his mouth.

Calm, calm, take the energy flowing through your body and push it to your brain.

"Peter, stop, try restarting. Shut everything down and try restarting."

The vehicle lurched to a halt and Gabriel and Misty flew forward in the water, slamming against the bulkhead. "Restarting, aye."

"Belay that!" Nerissa again. "Restarting the rover will take five minutes. Gabriel, do you have that much time?"

Burning and bubbling before his eyes. "No."

"Peter." Nerissa's voice was calm and smooth. "Look for Transfer, uh…" A few moments of thought, apparently. "Transfer Control. Select it, and tell me when you do."

The helmet cracked more and Misty screamed, "Come on!" as she tore away a worm, taking a chunk of the outer suit fabric with it.

"Guys?" Gabriel called.

"Transfer Auth Code?" Peter shouted. "I got a dialogue box!"

"OS188."

"OS1…"

"88!"

Peter shouted, "Okay, okay!"

A moment later Nerissa came back. "We have control of the rover. Blowing out air lock."

Water began to rush out as air came in, generators roaring all around them. When the water came down around Gabriel's ankles he called through the wall and into his earpiece, "Okay, we're standing in two inches of water here; you can open it."

"Opening air lock," Nerissa called, and the iris between them and the cockpit flew open. Peter turned around in the driver's seat as they tumbled in. Gabriel and Misty tore off their helmets.

"I'm sorry." Peter shook his head. "I couldn't blow the air lock…"

"Hey, you entered the code at the right time." Gabriel grabbed a pair of huge metal brushes. "Best you could do."

Misty tore off her suit and crawled out in a pair of shorts and a tank top as Gabriel did the same. They threw the suits, still smoking with worms, into the air lock. Gabriel hit a button next to Peter's head, and the iris closed as the suits began to turn the water on the other side to steam.

As the *Nebula* hauled the rover up, Gabriel spoke through the intercom. "Quarantine this vessel as soon as we're out of it." Outside, the smokers were receding in the distance as the *Nebula*'s underhull drew near.

Misty sat down and shook her fists in front of her face. "Is anything down here *not* going to try to *kill* us?"

"It's the *bottom of the ocean*!" Peter yelled. "We pick the *worst* friends."

Nerissa called to Gabriel through his earpiece as they all climbed out and crew members ran over to look after the vehicle. "When you're ready, come up to the bridge... Something you need to see."

"What, something else?"

"Something on the sonar."

When they reached the bridge, the *Nebula* was still moving away from the Smokers, but Nerissa was pointing over a small ridge into a valley beyond. As they moved toward it, they could see the valley was only about a mile wide. "If you look on the infrared, you can see the seepage here."

"Seepage?" Misty rubbed her elbow and stretched her

arms. Just moments before they had been running for their lives, and now they were expected to look at whatever Nerissa found interesting.

"Petroleum seepage. Down here in the cold deep, there are lots of naturally occurring oil wells, basically. Oil just seeps into the water. Some of the creatures live on it." She switched the image to the ocean floor, dark and shadowy and dotted with tree-sized weeds.

"Really? There are creatures that live on oil?"

"Petroleum is a fossil liquid. It's biological. So like everything else, something out there eats it."

Gabriel nodded. "Okay, but what was it—"

And then they turned on the floodlights. Gabriel saw movement that he could barely make out amid the flowing weeds. But then he saw tentacles and a squidlike body dart up and then down along the bottom, chasing after—something.

Nerissa swept her hand. "Our Lodger friends are on a rich petroleum vein."

Gabriel spotted another and another. Not as big as the ones they'd seen up above, but on the way. The size of cars, some of them wearing old shells on parts of their bodies.

"How many are there?" Gabriel asked.

"I see hundreds," Misty whispered. "Not as big, not grown, but... You know what this is?"

Gabriel did. "It's a Lodger nursery."

22

BACK AT NEMOLAB, Gabriel took the marker to the whiteboard as his crew and his family gathered in the bio-synthetics lab.

"So what do we know?"

"Hang on." Gabriel's mom held Peter and Misty at arm's length. "A little rough?"

"We made it," Gabriel said. "Everyone performed at the top of their capability."

"Rough, though?"

Misty took Mom's hands. "If I stopped to think about that, I think I'd go hide in my room."

"Is everyone done congratulating themselves?" Nerissa asked. "Gabe, get on with it."

Misty let Mom's hands go and looked toward Gabriel. "Start with the Lodgers."

Gabriel wrote down *LODGERS*.

Peter hung back, opposite Nerissa, and Gabriel thought both of them looked disturbed. Dark clouds of guilt covered Peter's face. *It wasn't your fault that it was hard to get the hatch open*, Gabriel wanted to say, but he was sure it would only sound insulting.

"Crustacean, with hermit tendencies. They take on shells," Nerissa said.

BIG SHELLS

"Draw an arrow to 'worms,'" Gabriel's mom suggested.

→ WORMS

Gabriel looked at the word *WORMS* and wrote *SYMBIOTIC* over the arrow. "Peter?"

"Well, now we know they eat oil."

PETROLEUM EATING

"So." Misty folded one arm across her body as she put her other hand under her chin. "The Lodgers are born in the valley of oil we saw. And they look for shells. But they're big, so they wind up scrounging and finding old mechanical stuff."

"They probably started working with the tube worms years ago. Maybe hundreds of years," Gabriel's dad said. "I mean, strictly speaking, it's a new species of worm. Superficially it looks like a tube worm, white with the reddish head, but there's a very curious adaptation where it can produce great heat, enough to burn other matter."

Gabriel nodded. "It seems like it should be impossible, but we've seen it happen." They'd left a handful of the worms in the back of the rover, and everyone was treating the worms with great care now.

Misty squinted. "It's not that impossible. Fireflies create a chemical reaction that burns on a very small scale. This is much the same."

Mom went to the whiteboard. "So we begin to have a picture of their life cycle. These develop as the worms, and they match up with the Lodgers, but... why are they coming up now?"

"Something would have to have changed," Misty answered.

"Remember the turtles we learned about in school?" Peter asked.

"Yeah," Gabriel said. "Sea turtles in California lay their eggs in the sand of the beach. When the babies are born, instinct tells them to travel toward the flashing lights—the sun on the ocean. But at night, the highway flashes, too, so they can crawl the wrong way."

"And die," Misty said.

"What if..." Gabriel began, and then paused to collect his thoughts. "What if they're swimming up to the Garbage Patch because there's so much oil there?" He drew a line at the bottom of the board to represent the seafloor and a bunch of ovals to represent the Lodgers. Then he drew a mess of dots up top—the garbage—and an arrow pointing from the Lodgers to the garbage.

Nerissa nodded. "The garbage would be very rich in petroleum. Like power pellets, they could sweep them up in their teeth the way whales do plankton."

"And once they have a taste for it," Gabriel added, "it's their new food source. Maybe a stronger source, better than seeping petroleum."

"That also explains a lot more about all the ships they take on." Peter got up, excited. "The Great Pacific Garbage Patch is gathered by the North Pacific Gyre. That's a current strong enough to slowly gather everything in the ocean—it'll push all those wrecks together—" Peter took the marker from Gabriel. "Right here." He drew an arrow straight down from the Garbage Patch to the seafloor.

"So they have everything they need. Food and Lodging."

"And the navy," said Nerissa.

Gabriel took back the marker and drew a little ship near the Garbage Patch. "Yeah. They've found the perfect habitat, except that it's the most dangerous place in the world for them. They're gonna keep going there today, and tomorrow, and the next day. Forever, until the navy blows them out of the water."

Nerissa raised a hand. "That's another problem. They're

eating petroleum? Filled with oil? It could be very bad to blow one up."

"What are you saying?" Misty asked.

"I'm saying US Navy carrier groups don't just use torpedoes; they use missiles three, *four* times stronger," Nerissa said. "If they hit one of the Lodgers, one of the big ones...the explosion could be enormous. Dangerous for every ship around."

Gabriel let that sink in. "And they don't know."

"Nope."

"Well," Misty said. "We're running out of time. Tomorrow is Saturday."

"Then we've got to meet them before they reach the ships." Gabriel capped the marker. "If we're going to save both the Lodgers *and* the navy, we have to draw the Lodgers away to a new habitat."

Gabriel's dad looked at the whiteboard. "Then let that be where we come in. You bring the herd. We'll make a pasture."

A sound emanated from the walls. *Fwooooooowwwwww.* So loud the walls shook. Gabriel looked up in shock. "That wasn't from any speaker."

"Doctors!" came the voice of the officer at the observation post. "We have visitors!"

Then they heard an answering sound, the Lodger down the corridor letting burst a trilling *fwowowowwowowow.*

Then the walls shook again, different and harder this time.

Dad looked up. "Something hit us."

Nerissa broke into a run immediately, and they all followed.

They reached the observation deck and looked out at the dome, where a World War II battleship was trying to bite its way into the city under the sea.

23

"**HOW MANY OF** them are there?" Gabriel shouted. He could see the battleship, bigger than the *Nebula* and broken into sections that twisted like a great barracuda, its teeth gnawing close to the dome. There were others behind it, but he couldn't see how many. A German submarine, tentacles swimming under it, swooped and nearly collided with the *Obscure*, still parked at its spot on the pad. Silver Lodger jet planes zipped up and over the battleship and under a wooden frigate with its masts and sails trailing behind it.

Fwooooowwwwooow. The battleship reared back and thrummed, shaking the whole of the dome, and then it whipped its tentacles and bashed the Nemoglass.

"Can we withstand that?" Gabriel's dad asked.

The officer turned to a console. "Structural integrity at ninety-six. It's cracking the dome."

That was incredible. The domes were built of the same Nemoglass that made up the windows of the *Obscure*.

"How did it hear?" Gabriel asked.

Nerissa considered. "There's no telling. Sea creatures can hear one another from miles away. It's even possible that thing you rigged up sends an even stronger pulse."

"What does it want?"

"We know what they want," Gabriel said. "The Lodger."

Now a cloud of dust whipped up outside on the ocean floor, beyond the pads where the *Nebula* and the *Obscure* sat, and a wave of new creatures began to arrive, thrumming one and all, the vibration filling Gabriel's ears. A living Russian MiG plane bounced along the hull of the *Nebula* and went over the side, crawling on the seabed toward a structure near the dome. When it reached it, it started hammering the walls with its landing gear.

"Security!" Dad called into a console. "Submersibles deploy to main dome and repel attackers."

"You have security?" Misty asked. "I thought there were only a few people here."

Nerissa scoffed. "Drones. We don't have an army. All we have are a few robots with small weapons."

Gabriel looked at his sister. "We have to let the Lodger go."

Down below the observation deck, drone submersibles

were coming around the dome as Gabriel and his sister ran. The cloud of dust began to kick up, obscuring the whole area. They were in a storm of sea dust now as another ram from the battleship sent shocks through the dome.

Gabriel looked back as he ran with Nerissa. "Misty and Peter—uh, you should head for the landing pad tube, for the *Obscure*. We may need to move the ship."

"Do you want us to wait for you?" Misty asked.

"I don't know—get her started and I'll try to get there as soon as I can."

"Wait," Peter said as he chased after Gabriel.

Misty stopped at the turn at the end of the corridor. "Are you coming?"

"In a second. We left the Crabsiren by the window. Maybe we can use it," Peter said insistently as Misty disappeared. They reached the one-way mirror and found the Lodger flying through the water in its tank-dome, feeling along the sides.

Peter picked up the Crabsiren. "Where do we aim it? The Lodger's in the dome, but maybe we could lead it somewhere."

Gabriel looked at the device in Peter's hand and wasn't sure they should be using it at all, now. It seemed to have called a bunch of those things right to them. "Why doesn't it just *burn* through?"

Nerissa shook her head. "Even if it can, I think it doesn't recognize *glass*."

"We have to get it out of there," Peter said, pointing at the Lodger's dome on the other side of the mirror. The lab shook as more Lodgers bashed against the buildings. Through the Lodger's dome, they could see a battleship Lodger battering against the Nemoglass. "Even if that thing breaks through the Lodger's dome, you still have all the others trying to wreck the place."

"Is there an air lock to this dome?" Gabriel asked.

"No," Nerissa said. "The only way in was where the drones sealed it off." This one was special and expanded in a hurry.

Gabriel called into his mic, "Mom, can you send the welder drones to open the Lodger's dome?"

"Negative," his dad's voice came back. "All the drones are out on defense."

"Okay." Gabriel tapped the mirror. "We have to go through here."

Peter sputtered. "What?"

"We get suits, you go back and seal this corridor, and we break this mirror open. It should be the weakest point. We swim out...uh, avoid the Lodger, we use welding torches..."

Nerissa waved her hand insistently as if to shush him. "And you'll be instantly crushed by *water pressure*. You're on the floor of the ocean, remember?"

Gabriel slammed the glass with his fists. "I did this. Our invention did this—it *called* them."

"You don't know that," Nerissa said. "Gabriel, think. Next?"

"Use a torpedo, from the *Obscure*. That could bust a hole in the dome."

"And likely destroy the Lodger in the process."

"No, no, no," Gabriel said. "Pincer torpedoes. Electricity. We shoot the dome with a pincer charge; my torpedoes are built on the same principles that those Nemoglass panels are. We hit it, and reverse the charge that's holding them together."

Peter nodded. "Just like the magnets in the nets."

Gabriel spoke into his earpiece. "Misty, you there?"

Misty came on. "Copy. *Obscure*." She was on the bridge. Gabriel looked through the mirror and past the Lodger, out to where the *Obscure* lay moored on the floor. "I just got here. Peter, you're supposed to be here."

"Dad, you in the control room?"

"Here," came Dad's voice.

Gabriel thought. "Send Misty the exact frequency of the charges the welders use to lock the Nemoglass panels into place. We're gonna have to shoot it."

"Whoa, whoa!" Misty shouted. "These aren't guided missiles, Gabriel. If it destroys that dome..."

"No, he's right." Gabriel's mom was talking and typing at the same time. "I'm sending the information to the *Obscure*."

"Bring torpedoes online," Gabriel ordered.

"Uh…torpedoes, aye." Misty sounded unsure.

"Does she know where the torpedoes are?" Nerissa asked.

"I know where they are!" Misty snarled. "I'm just not crazy about shooting one toward you." Her voice dropped. "Though I don't know *why*."

"You'll need to lift off the landing pad," Peter said. "And then swing left to point the ship at the dome."

"Bringing engines and torpedoes online." Blue-and-white lights began to glow along the hull of the ship.

"Did you get the info?"

"Got it. I'm entering that into the torpedo-control packets."

"We just took a hit in the dining hall," Gabriel's dad reported. "Sealing off galley and dining corridors."

"So much for the golden napkins," Nerissa said dryly.

"Argh!" Misty shouted.

"What?" Gabriel asked. He saw a Lodger shaped like a submarine pass over the *Obscure*, but it was headed for the domes.

"I can't lift off."

"You're still attached to the personnel tube!" Peter shouted. "Disengage the hull iris."

"Okay, okay."

After a moment they saw the *Obscure* lift off the floor of the ocean, exterior lights bathing the area beneath the ship as dust swirled in the water.

"Forty-five degrees left rudder," Gabriel ordered, and the ship began to turn. "Do you see the lower wall at the bottom of the other side of the dome?"

"I see a mirror down there."

"That's us." Gabriel tapped the glass and turned to Nerissa. "Do you think this wall—"

"Will keep standing when we *blow up the dome?*" Nerissa grabbed Gabriel and Peter and started walking them toward the door. "No, I do not."

"Fire!" Gabriel shouted as they ran down the corridor.

They reached the next door and swung it open as they heard Misty shout, "Torpedo away!"

Gabriel ran with Nerissa and Peter up a flight of stairs. As they reached the top, they felt a concussive force shake the walls. They poured into another corridor and kept running, stopping at the end to look through a window outside.

A ball of crackling arcs of energy was spreading along the far edge of the dome, bunching up where the dome was connected to the rest of the complex. Lights began to flicker all across the lab.

"Are you guys okay?"

"Okay," Gabriel said.

"Do you want to fire a second—"

And then it happened: Great tiles of Nemoglass began to fall from the study dome, shedding themselves like old skin.

"Yes!" Gabriel shouted. Then he remembered Misty had just asked a question. "I mean no! No second torpedo." A second one would come right through the lab wall, which Misty probably knew, but still.

The Lodger inside whipped its tentacles and soared into the ocean, nuzzling against a battleship Lodger that turned away from the main dome to run its tentacles over it.

"Now. Now you've got him, go."

But the attack did not let up. "I think they're mad." Gabriel looked down at Peter's hands, which still held the Crabsiren.

Okay.

"Peter, do you think we can put that thing to use on a lot of them?"

Peter's eyes grew wide and he shrugged. "I mean, I think we can try."

"Misty, can you re-engage with the iris and pick us up?"

Nerissa ran past him. "I'm headed for the *Nebula*." She disappeared down the hall.

They ran hundreds of yards down a corridor and heard an explosion as they reached the hangar. "That was a rocket-propelled grenade," Gabriel told Peter. "We shouldn't be shooting at them."

But that's the problem. They get themselves into situations where we have to defend ourselves.

Right?

They reached the tube into the *Obscure* and hurried onto the bridge, where Misty was standing next to Peter's station.

"Come on!" Misty shouted. "Here, Peter, helm's yours."

Peter sat immediately. "Disengaging iris. All engines online. We should thank your engineer guy."

Gabriel could feel the ship lifting away from the landing tube already, the whole onscreen front camera view obscured with kicked-up silt. They were spinning around, heading out toward the ocean. A smaller screen showed sonar thick with moving creatures.

Peter twisted the joystick. "Brace." The underside of an old ship came into view as they spun and soared under it. As the *Obscure* shot past, a passenger jet with teeth reared into the camera's view and bit at the lens, missed, and disappeared as they picked up speed.

"Um." Gabriel thought. "Can we broadcast the Crabsiren through the outside speakers?"

Peter looked at him. "If it were hooked up that way, I mean, sure."

"Yeah, we could use the forward speakers, aiming ahead of us. Take us beyond this group, hurry."

"Working on it." Peter maneuvered around the ships as the silt gave way to clear water. They scraped along the top of a submarine Lodger, and the whine of metal against metal shot through the whole ship.

Misty ripped open a panel and unscrewed some wires,

then pulled open the metal box that held the guts of the Crabsiren. "Peter?"

"Gabe, you wanna drive? Just continue this bearing," Peter said as he jumped from his console and ran to join Misty at the panels. Gabriel took his seat at the helm.

"Untwist the wires in the Crabsiren box," Misty told Peter. As Peter unscrewed the little yellow caps that held the wires in the Crabsiren together, Misty pulled out two large wires from the panel she was working at. "These should be the outside amplifiers." She held them out as Peter twisted the wires together and capped them. "Okay, hit it."

Suddenly the Crabsiren's high-pitched *fwowowowo-wowow* filled the air in the ship and the water around. "Come on, louder." Gabriel whipped his hands like a conductor.

"You should be thrilled we got this far," Misty said. "Louder, aye."

The *Obscure* kept moving, the ship shaking with the sound of the Crabsiren. "Come on, guys."

A battleship nearby turned toward them and emitted a massive call that rocked them to the side.

"Did it…?"

Peter looked up from the panel at the sonar map in the corner of the view screen as he ran back to his console. "Gabriel, here they come."

"Onscreen rear view."

And they were coming. Battleships, submarines, planes, they were coming, one after the other.

"Full speed ahead!" Gabriel shouted as a giant carrier with a mouth came closer. "Are they following or attacking?"

"You're asking me?" Peter sent them down and up again as the sound deafened them.

They kept driving the Lodgers, racing through clear ocean until Gabriel called out, "How far off from Nemolab are we?"

"Twenty miles," Peter said.

"Kill the siren," Gabriel called. "Get us out of here. Steer us wide and west. I don't want to sail through those things."

As they raced wide away, Misty reported from the sonar. "They're coming. I mean they're still looking for the source of the sound."

"Okay, we can't let them see us. Dive, dive, dive, right to the floor," Gabriel called.

Peter sent them twisting off at an odd angle, and they nearly scraped the floor as he twisted the ship down and under the school of Lodgers. "There's a canyon. I'm gonna take it."

"Go," Gabriel agreed. His stomach lurched as the ship whipped up and banked down into a rocky crevasse in the ocean floor. They traveled fast for a minute, cliffs on either side. "Easy."

Silence.

They had lost the Lodgers.

When they returned to Nemolab twenty minutes later, the assault was long over and replaced with a flurry of activity. Antennae were broken all over the seabed, and Gabriel could see walls of some of the outside structures lying in pieces as drones scurried about making repairs. Still more were swimming around the main dome with torches, looking for cracks.

Fabulous, Gabriel. You come home one day and wreck the place. And you're supposed to be the good *one.*

"Nice and steady," Gabriel said as they approached the landing pad for a second time. "Look at that."

He checked the date and time on the view screen's corner. "If the navy tries to destroy those things, I don't know how well they'll do."

Misty was silent for a while. "I agree."

Gabriel touched a communication button. "*Obscure*, coming home."

Gabriel's dad came on. "Welcome back. You did good."

But looking at the damage to Nemolab, Gabriel didn't think that was true at all.

24

THEY GATHERED IN the control room at the top of the Manta tower, where Gabriel's parents leaned against a wall of screens and buttons. Behind them the sea went on in its usual, colorful way as drones zipped around doing repair work on the glass.

"Look," Gabriel's dad said. "You got them away from the lab. None of us was hurt."

Gabriel wasn't feeling any better. "I think we just made things worse."

Dad seemed to see the pain on Gabriel's face and shook his head. "No. They got here awfully fast. I'm thinking even if your invention contributed, it didn't do so by much." He glanced at Peter and Misty. "And *you* two."

Peter and Misty looked up.

"I'm proud to call you friends."

Nerissa chortled. "Do their parents even know where they *are*?"

"Can we not talk about this right now?" Gabriel asked. Misty looked at him with sadness. He'd heard her clearly. She was done lying. This was her last trip. But he had no great desire to hear his sister jump all over him about it.

"Okay," Gabriel's mom said, "your father discovered something that he wants to share with you."

Gabriel's dad turned around and brought a sonar view of the Lodger attack up onscreen. They saw many shapes, some larger than others, from biplane to battleship. "Look at this one, on the upper right." He pointed at a submarine shape. He changed the view.

Now there was a diagram of expanding circles of white, coming from various points on the screen. All of the points of light were coming from the base. Except one. A pulsing burst of energy was emanating from the submarine Lodger Gabriel's dad had pointed out.

"What's that?" Gabriel asked.

"Radio signals. All of these on the bottom, those are us, sending lots of little signals to the drones, to equipment, to each other. That one—it's weaker, but it's constant."

"I don't understand." Misty stared. "A Lodger had a *radio*?"

"No." Gabriel stared at the image. He'd seen this before.

"Well, yes and no. It has a radio, but probably not on purpose. That's a tracker."

"Is it one of ours?" Nerissa asked.

"No."

"Navy?"

Gabriel's dad nodded. "I think that's why the carrier group has the confidence to plan an attack on the Lodgers. They tagged one, and now they can find them more easily."

"But... if they're following that ping," Peter reasoned, "they could know where *you* are."

Gabriel's dad thought. "Maybe. I doubt they could track it this far."

Gabriel's mom waved her hand. "Nemolab is a secret, but it's a secret plenty of people know. Especially in the navy."

"What the navy doesn't know is that we're trying to help the Lodgers," Gabriel said.

"And we're trying to help *them*," Nerissa said. "Don't forget that if they shoot those things, it'll be like setting off a bomb."

"Well, there is a bright side, though," Misty said.

"What's that?"

"Now that you've seen this," she said, "you can track them, too."

Nerissa pointed at Misty as if to say, *Yeah!* "She's right. We can track the Lodgers."

Gabriel was nodding. "So we have a way of tracking

the Lodgers and a way of directing them, at least in short bursts. That's what we need, right? Nerissa, how much time do we have to get them away from the naval attack?"

Nerissa said, "About fifteen hours."

"Then we need to hurry," Gabriel said. He looked down. His time at Nemolab was over again. "I'm sorry. We have to get going."

Twenty minutes later, Gabriel and his crew gathered with Nerissa and his parents at a branching corridor that led toward the two ships. Gabriel's mom had a black bag with the Nemo *N* on it, and she drew out gifts for each of them.

"Here," she said to Gabriel.

He looked down to see a light metal box and tilted it, looking at Peter, Misty, and Nerissa. Light from the windows in the junction where they stood glimmered off the metal. One way went back to the Manta tower, where Gabriel's dad was manning the controls. One way went toward the *Nebula*, and one toward the *Obscure*.

Gabriel unfastened the box and saw a bed of blue satin, within it a shining golden disk etched with numbers. It had a pair of hands like a clock.

"What is it?" Misty asked.

"It's an astrolabe," Gabriel said. "Ancient mariners used them to determine their position by the stars."

"It's the astrolabe from the *Nautilus*. Your dad thought it made sense for you to have it."

"Oh." He was shocked. The piece was priceless, but

what was striking Gabriel at just that moment was that his sister was right there. His sister, the oldest, who was as much a carrier of the Nemo vision as he was. More so, maybe.

"It's beautiful." Nerissa came to his shoulder. "It makes sense to have this on the *Obscure*."

He looked at Nerissa. "But…"

"We navigate as truly as we can. And I can't think of anyone trying to be more true to the best of Captain Nemo's philosophy than you. That's hard to admit, but it's true." She hugged Gabriel and their mom joined in, and they were locked together for a moment. All the madness and anger washed away and disappeared, just for a moment.

"Peter." Gabriel's mom pulled away and swiftly wiped a tear from her eye. "We weren't sure that it was a good idea for the *Obscure* to have a crew. But you're a fine helmsman, and you helped defend our home."

"Misty." Now Gabriel's mom clasped her hands in front of her. "I see how much you value the sea and its creatures. I don't have any more antiques, but I want both of you to have these." She reached into a pocket in her coat, pulled out a pair of black wristbands, and handed one to each.

"Whoa!" Misty exclaimed. "This is a…Nemotech receiver." She unclasped it, laying it over her wrist. It was exactly like the ones Gabriel and Nerissa wore. "This works with our earbuds?"

"An upgrade," Gabriel's mom said.

"So this, what, tracks my steps?" Peter smiled.

"If you're into that, yes." Gabriel laughed. "But most of all it connects you to Nemolab. It'll transmit your position, and if need be you can call any of us for help."

"Although lately you've been more help to us than the other way around. I don't know." Mom's eyes crinkled marvelously. "I just thought it would be nice to have you connected."

She kissed each of them on the forehead, then stepped back and cleared her throat.

Nerissa looked at her own wrist. "Ticktock. We have to get out to open sea."

Mom wobbled her head, *la-di-da*. "Oh, you don't want your gift?"

Nerissa sighed. "Sure, Mom. What did you get for me?"

"Actually it's something I wanted to hand over." Mom pulled a smooth stone about the size of her thumb from the bag.

Nerissa took it and turned it around. "What is this?"

"It's a hard drive. You can only access it on your ship. Everything we know about the location of the *Nautilus* is on there. It's a jumble. Some strange stuff, some clues that turned up in Europe...anyway. It would mean a lot to your father if you looked for the ship. If you could find the time." She shrugged. "I know you're busy."

"Check it out, Gabe. I got a scavenger hunt." Nerissa turned over the stone, smiling. She slipped it into her pocket and hugged her mom.

Mom kissed her forehead as she had Gabriel's and said, "You know what you're doing? At least right now?"

"Always do." Nerissa smiled briefly.

Gabriel said, "If everything we've theorized is right, we'll locate the Lodgers, the largest school of them, around the Garbage Patch. If we have to talk to the navy before we can round up the Lodgers and lead them off, we will."

"Be careful," Gabriel's mom said. "Sometimes they don't want to talk."

That seriousness of getting in the way of the US Navy sank in for a moment and Gabriel felt a tiny burst of panic, like a far-off creature growling from over the horizon. "One thing at a time," Gabriel said.

He hugged his mom one more time, smelling her hair, and then broke off. He gestured to Misty and Peter and ran ahead of them toward the *Obscure*. He didn't look at anybody, because he was holding back tears.

∿∿

At sixty knots the *Obscure* quickly left Nemolab behind. Gabriel stood at the view screen, which had been split into three: sonar, aft, and forward. The *Nebula* raced ahead of them, climbing the shelf and disappearing into the tunnel that would empty out at the Dakkar Curtain like water through a grate.

Behind the *Nebula* by several lengths, the *Obscure* entered the rock tunnel.

For a moment Gabriel was seized by claustrophobia as

the rocks swooped all around them. The *Obscure* sailed steady and true. "Good job, Peter." Up ahead, past the *Nebula*, he saw great mountainous columns coming miles off. "You ready for the Curtain?"

"I'm fine, but you should sit down and strap in." They would have to turn on their sides slightly. Gabriel nodded and got in the captain's chair, pulling a safety belt over his shoulders.

"*Nebula* approaching the curtain," came Nerissa's voice over the intercom. He could see the giant sub already starting to list to starboard, and he pictured hundreds of sailors hanging on to pipes and handholds, only some of them strapping in. It would be like tilting a building on its side. "Exiting the tunnel in thirty seconds."

"*Nebula* is through the Curtain," Nerissa called. "Open sea and bearing east."

"Our turn," Peter said.

"Steady."

"Brace." They rolled to starboard, the *Obscure* turning on its side as the rocky columns rushed toward them.

Volcanic rock slid by outside the windows of the ship, thankfully farther away than the *Nebula* had to deal with. He counted silently as they went, waiting for the other side.

The rocks opened up, and the sea revealed itself beyond. "We're clear."

Excellent.

25

AN HOUR LATER they heard the ships. An American came on the radio.

"All ships prepare for encounter. Time to meet estimated twenty-five minutes."

Encounter. Gabriel knew that could mean only one thing: attack.

"I found the carrier group." Peter threw the sonar image up onscreen. Gabriel could see forty ships coming westward toward the beeping tic–marked Platform Island. "And there are the Lodgers." The Lodgers were a fleet unto themselves, moving fast. A mass close together.

"How long till we catch them?"

"At this speed, ten minutes."

"Make it five. Full speed."

"What are you going to do?"

Yeah, what are you going to do?

The only thing to do was try to talk. "Misty, can you open that channel? Can I talk to the navy?"

Misty shrugged. "Sure." After a moment she said, "Oookay."

Gabriel walked back to his chair. "This is Gabriel Nemo, Captain, Nemotech Submarine *Obscure*, calling lead ship, advancing fleet US Navy."

There was no answer. Gabriel saw shapes far ahead, and Misty magnified them. He saw the undulating tentacles of a Lodger in a Vietnam-era battleship.

"Three minutes to meet them," Peter reported.

Gabriel nodded. "I say again, US Navy, this is…"

"This is Admiral Waring, Carrier USS *Dubois*… *Obscure*, state your purpose."

He had them. But what to tell them? "We are tracking…a large group of sea creatures, whales, whalelike creatures, headed your way. We wanted to warn you. So you can avoid collision." He shrugged at Misty.

"We know what they are, Captain Nemo," came the voice. "They're sinking ships. You know we can't let that go on."

"You're making a mistake!" Gabriel shouted. "If you antagonize these creatures…"

"If *you* are not controlling them, then you should heave off."

"We're *not*, but *listen*. They're basically giant moving oil tankers. If you fire on them, you'll be sorry."

"It could be thirty minutes to catch them," Peter whispered.

"Give me a chance, Admiral. You have to trust me."

"You know that's not how it works," the voice came back. "They've sunk ships. There's no trust here."

Gabriel turned to the rest. "Thirty minutes?"

Peter nodded. "Just about."

"Keep moving. No, wait." Gabriel held up a hand. He was thinking of Nerissa, folding her arms and chastising him. And Misty's trust that he would do the right thing. Suddenly the right thing seemed clear.

Peter was still waiting. "You want to *stop?*"

"I just…" He looked from Misty to Peter. "Okay, listen."

Peter took his hands off the controls and took out his earpiece. Misty leaned against her console.

"Okay. Here's the thing. We're riding now directly toward a CBG; that's a carrier battle group. You're talking an aircraft carrier, probably a couple of destroyers, and probably a supply ship with advanced sonar. Not to mention helicopters whose only purpose—whose *only* purpose—is to spot submarines. We replaced the escape dinghy at Nemolab. It can go as far as you like…"

"Gabe." Peter shook his head.

"*Listen*." They had to hear this. "We have only

electrical weapons. And we have every reason to think that the navy will fire on us. What I'm telling you is that this is my fight. I can man this ship by myself—it was designed that way."

"Can you man it *well*?" Misty asked.

Gabriel sighed. It would be better with them. He could lie to himself and say that he would do better without worrying about them, but the truth was that he did need a crew. But what if they got hurt?

"It won't matter if they shoot the *Obscure* with guided missiles. What I'm suggesting is that you and Peter take the dinghy now, and head for California. I got you into this, and I can't... what Misty said is right."

"What did Misty say?" Peter asked.

"She said you couldn't possibly have told your parents how dangerous this would be, because you didn't know."

"*You* didn't know, either," Misty observed. "And I already said I'm in it for the Lodgers."

"Oh, come on. I can't have it on my conscience if we sink."

"Then *don't sink*," Peter scoffed. "Because you're crazy if you think I'm getting in the escape dinghy now."

Misty crossed her arms. "Gabriel, you're not forcing us. I can't speak for Peter, but this is the mission. I am here for the mission. And... I'm staying."

"She can speak for me if she wants."

"And we know some neat tricks. I think we're better here."

"You can't know that."

"Oh, come on—look, time's up." Misty clapped her hands. "You've made your speech, and you've made us aware that we're in danger. Now, as far as I can tell, we don't have time to go over it again."

"But—"

She cleared her throat. "Let's try this. Gabe, you want to ask us one more time if we want to get off?"

"Uh..." He wasn't following her.

"The words you're looking for are, '*Would you like to leave?*'"

Fine. "Would you like to lea—"

"No!" they both shouted.

Misty stamped her foot. "Now, what're your orders?"

He was lucky to have them in his life. They loved the life—

"*Obscure?*" came Nerissa's voice. "We've spotted the Lodgers."

Peter looked back at him, and Gabriel flicked his hand at the screen. Peter put up the sonar screen.

"There they are," Peter said. A mass of spots on the sonar image, some as small as the biplane and some as large as the British man-of-war, were amassed and traveling west toward the center of the Garbage Patch. They'd caught them.

"We have a feed from Bubo 4," Nerissa announced over the intercom.

Peter called for the feed, and the upper half of the view screen filled with an image of the ocean shot from a drone flying overhead at several thousand feet. They could see faint shadows under the water, and then the Lodgers emerged—submarines and old ships shooting from the water before diving back. They could hear the sound of wind buffeting the drone.

A loud roar split the air and the image shook. The camera on the drone shifted up as another roar came fast, with a plane in view this time: A sleek white jet flew about a thousand feet above the drone, threatening to crack the microphones with its engine roar.

"What was that?"

"I've seen that." Misty put her palm her forehead. "My mom loves them. That was a Boeing F/A 18E/F Super Hornet. It would have to have come from a carrier."

"Nerissa, you copy that?" Gabriel called.

"Copy. It must be looking for the Lodgers. And if we've spotted them, they have."

"Show us the carrier group?"

The image craned forward and zoomed in. They could see a line of ships far off the horizon. There was a carrier—that would have been the ship that Gabriel was talking to earlier, and he reminded himself the admiral was named Waring and he had better be ready to talk to him again. Plus two more ships on either side. And a helicopter zipping around.

Another loud engine screamed past the Bubo and flew by.

Gabriel took it in and nodded. "Okay, we have the Crabsiren, and our goal is to get the Lodgers away and not get hit by *anything*. And we don't have much to defend ourselves with."

"Do you want to ask Nerissa for some *real* torpedoes?" Misty asked. "There might be time."

"No . . . Let's face it, it would be a mistake to fire a missile at a navy ship. Even pincers, which at most do electrical damage. That would be . . . that would be *it*. Every ship would fire on us."

"So what's left? If we're gonna travel with no weapons."

Gabriel thought, looking out at the water swirling with plastic. They were inside the Garbage Patch now. Very soon they would meet the enemy. "Buoys."

"Sonar buoys?" Peter asked. "What for?"

"How many do we have?"

Misty tapped at her console. "We have five sonar buoys—they're in the aft section below, science tube."

"Peter, keep on this heading. Misty, let's go find the buoys. We'll need some tools."

Gabriel and Misty hurried back through the passenger section but stopped short of the dive room, dropping down through a hatch in the floor and heading toward the engine room. Behind the engine room was a room for prepping and deploying sensors and buoys.

Gabriel bent his head to avoid the low ceiling and peered at a stack of metal shelves. Stacked neatly and secured were large, round buoys that reminded him of giant clams about four feet wide and three feet tall. Gabriel rolled the first one out on a wheeled cart and put his hands on the sides.

When the buoy went in the water, it would send a radio signal back to Misty's console. You could let it float fifty miles away and still get a signal, the only problem being that you either had to attach a cable to it to bring it back, or you had to go get it later.

"Here, let's grab the rest," he told her. He and Misty rolled out the next four and let them rest against the wall next to a small hoist to lift the buoys into the torpedo tube.

They sat on the metal floor, looking at the buoys, and Gabriel grabbed a drill. He looked for the rivets in a panel on the side of the buoy, right below the *N* swirl. He opened it up and Misty looked in beside him.

"So what are we doing?" Misty asked.

"We need to be able to stop the navy before they get themselves blown up, and we can't shoot them. So we're gonna open up these sonar buoys and convert them from sound-listening devices into static-electricity amplifiers. Strong enough to stop a ship in its tracks, at least until we get the Lodgers away."

"Static-electricity amplifier, huh? Wow." Misty looked at the opened buoy. "An electromagnetic pulse. You're building an EMP device."

"Well," Gabriel said, "*we* are."

By the time they had the devices converted, Peter was calling them back to the bridge, because the ships were getting close.

～✓

"Oh, boy," Gabriel said. The sonar screen now showed the playing board: The naval ships were farthest away from the *Obscure*, coming west. The Lodgers continued east, leaping their way toward the center of the Patch and the ships. And the *Obscure* was still trailing the Lodgers by miles.

But where—

"Where's Nerissa?"

"I don't have her on sonar," Peter said.

"Well, she didn't run away, so she's gone quiet." Gabriel didn't like not knowing where his sister was. "This is getting dangerous."

"What do you want to do?" Peter asked.

"Uh...give me the US Navy frequency."

"Got it," Misty said.

When she opened the channel he said, "*Obscure* to

Admiral Waring. We've found them, we've spotted the Lodgers, and we request permission to corral them and lead them away."

"We have, too," Waring said. "They're exactly where they're supposed to be."

"Admiral, I say again, if you shoot them, you will take extensive damage. They are highly volatile, like...shooting an oil tanker volatile. It would be like shooting a bomb."

"You need to clear off. Is that you in the submarine?"

Gabriel was about to say *yes* when Nerissa came online. "No, sir. That's me."

The *Nebula* appeared on the sonar screen. She had dived deep and come around the Lodgers to put herself between them and the navy.

"Who's that?" Waring asked.

"*Nebula*. Check your files. I can wait." Onscreen, the *Nebula* surfaced, right in the center of the Garbage Patch, not far from the Lodgers. There was a chuckle in her voice as she said, "Boys."

"Torpedo in the water!" Peter shouted. A white missile burst from underneath the *Nebula* and shot across the water, far clear of the Americans but in their direction. A shot across the bow, but *still*.

Gabriel jumped on the intercom and howled, "What are you *doing*?"

"Gabe, trust me. It's a warning shot."

"Return fire!" Waring ordered.

"Wait!" Gabriel shouted. "That was a warning shot! A warning shot!"

A large helicopter zipped from somewhere behind the carrier and dropped a payload that hit the water with a splash. *Nebula* was already diving, and when the torpedo hit the water about two hundred yards from her position, the *Nebula* was gone.

"Halt! You are under arrest!" came Waring's voice.

"Going silent," Nerissa said quickly. "Finish the job." And then she was gone.

Horns rang out as a quarter of the ships broke off, following Nerissa's direction.

"*Obscure*," Waring said as he came back on. "We don't have any arrest warrant on file for you. So this is your last warning."

"Admiral, *please*! I can drive the creatures off to someplace safe." He turned back to Peter. "Are we caught up to the Lodgers enough to use the Crabsiren?"

Peter flipped on the front camera and they saw a twisting, living 747 flying through the water behind a tentacled battleship. "Half a mile away."

"How far are they from the navy?"

"Another five miles."

"Start the Crabsiren," Gabriel ordered. "A two-second blast."

A loud, piercing trill shot from the speakers of the *Obscure*, emanating toward the Lodgers. He saw the submarine creature in the end of the procession look back as if surprised.

"We've got to get in front of them. Shut it off." Peter doused it.

"We are receiving your message to the creatures," Waring said. "Back down or you will be fired upon."

"I'm *trying to lead them away*," Gabriel answered. "You guys need to halt, and I can take care of this." He keyed the mic off and turned to Peter. "Dive deep, then under the Lodgers, and up. Put us between the Lodgers and the navy."

"Aye, Captain."

The ship tilted sharply and they dove, dropping down hundreds of feet as streams of tiny plastic ran over the screen.

"Fire the Crabsiren again, two-second burst. Aim it down. I don't want the Lodgers to be surprised when we show up again."

Peter nodded and blew the horn again, two seconds, and shut it off as they dived. After about thirty seconds they leveled off and Peter listened.

"The water's a whole lot colder down here. The layer of cold water will be like ... a blanket; the sonar from the carrier won't be able to reach us down here. We'll be invisible to the ships above."

For several seconds they traveled toward the shapes

on the sonar, passing under the family of Lodgers, which Gabriel counted to be about thirty. The navy ships were above and forward another couple of miles.

Peter gasped suddenly.

"What?" Misty asked.

Peter pointed at the sonar, which suddenly lit up with a single other shape. "We're not alone. There's another ship down here."

"Onscreen."

The rearview cameras filled the screen. Coming up fast was a shape like the nose of a whale.

And it kept coming, flowing into view, an enormous gray submarine. Across its nose were the words US NAVY and a name: USS *ALASKA*.

"Oh my," Misty said. "It's an Ohio."

Gabriel blinked. "Yes, it is." Ohio class, that was. Biggest submarines in the US fleet. Five hundred and sixty feet long. Forty-two feet wide. And equipped with a full battery of six fifty-pound, twenty-one-inch-wide guided torpedoes. Plus a nuke or two.

And it had taken Gabriel's dive as an act of aggression. Warnings were over.

An explosion of air burst from below the ship, and Gabriel saw the shape hurtling toward them even before Peter shouted.

"Torpedo in the water!"

26

THE SOUND OF the sonar echoing off the torpedo beeped loudly, growing in intensity.

"Evasive maneuvers, hard right rudder, dive!" Gabriel shouted. "Fire countermeasures."

"Countermeasures, aye," Misty repeated.

"Dive, aye!" Peter shouted. The *Obscure* turned on its side as it dropped and slid to the right.

Onscreen, from housings on the left and right sides of the *Obscure*, small barrels fired off and propelled themselves into the water. Each one had a loud, rattling screw, kicking up clouds of bubbles as they shot out, putting themselves in the path of the oncoming missile.

The torpedo sliced through the top of the first's cloud

but caught the second like a scent, turning to charge. It closed on the barrel.

An explosion split open the water and rocked the *Obscure* as they completed their dive, curving around.

"What now?" Misty shouted.

I have no idea! I've never gone to war with the US Navy before! Gabriel wanted to shout back. Instead he asked, "Ideas? We could run."

"Ram them," Peter said. "This is a Nemoship; you could ram them."

"I don't know if we'd survive that. They might be expecting that—that ship looks big enough to battle the *Nebula*. And ... you're talking about sending a lot of people into the water."

"Use the EMP buoys," Misty offered.

"Right, right!" Gabriel pointed, nodding. "And Peter, you're onto something. We can't ram them—but we can get close."

"*Torpedo in the water!*" Peter shouted, his hand to his earpiece.

The missile dropped from below the great ship. The alarm system howled as the torpedo closed in, now two hundred yards away.

"Hard left, ascend, countermeasures!" Gabriel shouted.

"Countermeasures away," Misty said, and the barrels shot out. He saw the missile catch the little barrels and crack up, sending shock waves through the water. The *Obscure* shook in the water as it rose and they leveled off. Gabriel tightened the safety harness of his seat.

"Gabe," Misty said, "that's it, we're out of counter-measures."

"Okay, okay. Peter, can you get us right under the *Alaska?*"

"I don't know, sure. How close? Their port torpedo tube door just opened!" Peter shouted.

"I mean close, hug them—dive down and get right underneath them. So close we almost touch." There could be another torpedo at any second. "Hurry."

"Aye," Peter said. The *Alaska* grew in their view as Peter made the engines roar. The nose of the navy ship loomed as they got closer. Rivets and seams on the submarine were visible now.

"Closing on the *Alaska*. Wait. Torpedo in the water!"

"Close in!"

The missile shot out as the *Alaska* grew, its nose disappearing from view. Now a long section of the middle of the ship filled the screen. The torpedo shot past the *Obscure*, not even slowing down for them, too close to lock on.

"Hard left rudder, dive forty feet, full stop right under!" Gabriel rattled off.

"Just don't collide with it!" Misty yelled.

"Hard left, dive forty!" Peter shouted, yanking at the

controls. The *Obscure* dipped, spinning hard left as Gabriel's body pressed against his safety straps.

"Full stop!" Peter cried, as the stabilizers howled and they came to a halt under the naval submarine. It looked like a vast column directly over them, still moving, ten times the size of the *Obscure*.

"Okay," Gabriel said, looking up at the ceiling. "Chances are they haven't yet figured out where we went. Flank speed, stay right with it. Prepare to release science payload."

"Flank speed."

"On my mark, slow one third, deploy payload, and then dive, full speed. We'll go *down*, the buoy will go *up*. Right into them."

"On your mark." Peter watched the screen, his hands on the controls.

Gabriel was watching the underside of the ship. "Slow one third."

The diving fins spun and the *Obscure* lurched as it slowed; the *Alaska* seemed to speed up onscreen. They had to fire and then get out of the way—both of their own buoy and of the giant submarine's engines. Gabriel watched the shape passing on the sonar screen. *Tick. Tick.*

"Deploy payload."

"Deploy, aye."

On a new section of the screen, a camera hanging over

the back of the *Obscure* watched the door open and one of the large buoys shoot out, tumbling into the water. It spun and bounced behind them along the underside of the *Alaska*.

"Dive full speed, punch down!"

"Full speed dive!" Peter yanked the controls back. "Hang on." They lurched hard, the walls filling with water as the nose pointed toward the depths.

Gabriel grabbed onto his chair as his legs dangled toward the view screen. Misty and Peter held on to their controls, each of them pressing their body against their own console. "Fire!" Gabriel shouted.

"Firing buoy!" Peter yelled as he punched a button.

On the screen, the buoy beeped like a contented little creature, bouncing along the bottom of the *Alaska*. Then just as it reached the end of the sub, it flashed.

Brilliant light filled the screen for a moment, and the beeping stopped. As the light faded, the buoy tumbled away, dead.

"Well?" Misty asked.

"Level off." Gabriel looked around. "Did we take any damage?"

"Leveling off," Peter said. "No, we were far enough away." Then he grinned. "That was pretty cool."

"Did the *Alaska*?" He could see the big sub still moving forward. How would they tell if it had been affected?

But the vessel was slowing, lurching away from them about half a mile above.

Peter pointed. The currents of the ocean caught the big ship and it turned on its side, clumsily sliding and twisting. "I think they're disabled."

Misty put her hand to her mouth. "Gabriel, you don't think we hurt them? I mean the people?"

"No, no, it should be temporary." Gabriel shook his head. "But they won't be chasing us for now. Let's surface. It's time to save the Lodgers."

27

THE *OBSCURE* ROSE quickly. But for what seemed like minutes, the sonar stayed blank and they couldn't see where the Lodgers or the navy were at all. There might have already been shelling, death, maybe even multiple casualties. Then as they rose, the images flickered to life on the sonar screen.

"There's the Lodgers." Peter indicated a group of large spots, more or less still in one place. They might be moving about, but onscreen they were not leaving their area.

"And there's the navy." Misty nodded toward the carrier battle group, coming fast as it crossed the ocean.

"Any sign of the ships that peeled off?"

"No. Still hunting Nerissa, I guess," Peter said. "I hope she's okay."

"Me, too." Gabriel shook his head. "But she asked us to do this. How far is the navy group from the Lodgers?"

"Just about three miles."

"That's close enough to hit the Lodgers with a missile, if the navy wants," Misty observed. "They could use ballistic missiles or shoot the Lodgers from the planes."

"If we race up and put ourselves in front of the battle group . . . call the *Lodgers*. We have the Crabsiren; we know it worked once. Call them. Now, short bursts. Aim for their group. Head toward the Lodgers. Ignore the navy for now, ascend flank speed, and turn on the siren."

"Ascending flank speed, heading for the Lodgers, aye." He flipped a switch, and a howling song shot out from the nose of the *Obscure*. "Siren."

"Turn on our front lights, high beam," Gabriel ordered. "Put a long white line right on the Lodger group."

Onscreen, a brilliant white beam shot forward ahead of them in the water, lighting up tiny swirls of plastic in the ocean. They sped upward, still seeing nothing but the light in blackness. The siren howled ahead of them. They were lighting a path straight to the Lodgers.

Misty said, "Gabriel, if the navy has more subs or drones underneath, they might see us. I mean, we're lit up like a Christmas tree."

"We have to take that chance. Right now, our only interest is getting the attention of the Lodgers."

They continued upward another fifty, another hundred

feet, and then the first Lodger came into view. It was an old battleship, dancing in the water, its great mouth open as it ate, and swam, and ate.

Another Lodger, a World War II frigate, skinny and tall, dove under the battleship and up, nudging it and sailing through the plastic. There were more besides.

"They remind me of..."

"Dolphins." Misty read his mind. "Or whales. Just... feeding in the Garbage Patch. Playing, even. That's what they're doing. Just living their lives."

"Yeah. But they picked the wrong home. Peter, level off and slow. Can you oscillate the horn, blast and then taper, then blast again?"

The whine of the siren stopped and started again, blasting out, and out, and out.

"What if they don't want to leave?" Misty asked. "We don't know how they communicate. This is just a call; what if they're not interested? They have..."

On the view screen, the battleship dipped its eyes down, swiveling until it saw the *Obscure*'s beam. Then it shrugged its weight and turned its whole body, moving in ways a battleship was never designed for.

"Slow due west, keep running the siren," Gabriel said. "Come on, guys. Follow the leader."

And then the battleship began to travel.

There was an explosion that shook the *Obscure* as a missile hit the water.

"Where was that?"

"Half a mile off," Peter said. "Warning shot. The navy group is nearly here."

"Come on!"

The tentacled frigate watched the battleship go and followed the beam of light and the siren. Then a submarine flicked its tail and followed, not far behind. Then another and another.

"They're following!" Misty shouted. "They're following!"

A great howling whine filled the bridge as the battleship Lodger called them, and the siren answered. Five more Lodgers fell into the group, moving west with the *Obscure*.

Another explosion rocked the sub from the surface.

"Okay." Gabriel turned to Peter and Misty. "Let's lead them west of here. But first, slide us right under the forward line of navy ships. Cut straight up."

The *Obscure* turned hard left and started cutting across the line of approaching ships.

"Release all science payloads," Gabriel said.

They heard the ratcheting against the hull of buoy after buoy, four in all, emerging from the back of the *Obscure* as the ship shot through the water. The buoys floated upward toward the surface, little blinking lights on the sonar screen.

"Admiral Waring?" Gabriel called.

"We see you," Waring said. "And you've fired on a US Navy vessel. That makes you ..."

"Technically, no, we fired no weapons," Gabriel said, then lower, "Peter, let's go."

He spoke into the radio again. "I just released some buoys." The buoys flashed on the surface, beeping. The *Obscure* was moving away, the Lodgers following.

"Surrender, *Obscure*. We will be over you in minutes."

You jerk! Gabriel wanted to shout. *Can't you see I'm trying to save you?* But he breathed. "Sir, the Nemo Foundation has taken custody of the Lodgers. We're moving them to a spot where they won't harm anyone. That's all I'm at liberty to say at the moment, but I don't think they'll be in these lanes again." Gabriel paused. "I promise, I promise, this is *way* better than the alternative."

Onscreen, he saw the underside of the oncoming ships' prows. He nodded to Peter. "Trigger the buoys."

On the surface there were four bursts, one after the other. He saw the underside of the explosions of energy, lightning zipping from one ship to another. A ball of static electricity swept across each nose as the water boiled.

Peter listened for a moment. "Their engines just died ... All of them."

Gabriel heard alarms ring out and then cut off. He waited for a second, half expecting that Waring would come back on the radio. But of course he couldn't, because all of the naval ships' radios were dead for a while, as well.

The prows were slowing, little lightning strikes still popping in the water.

They were silent for a moment, the three of them staring. Gabriel winced, overcome with sudden guilt that he had unleashed even a non-deadly weapon on manned ships.

"Now what?" Misty finally asked.

Now we sit here amazed that we didn't die. He wanted to go up and look from the surface but knew that would only be tempting fate. "Now we *run*."

Then the real journey began—the trek to the Lodgers' new home.

28

WHEN THE *OBSCURE'S* high beam finally hit the valley that Gabriel's parents had picked out, the water shimmered with plastic particles. As the ship traveled through them, the particles swirled, and the Lodgers munched. Mom had sent them the coordinates for this spot while they were on the way. As the Lodgers swam about in the valley, Mom and Dad came aboard from a Nemotech rover they had parked nearby.

Gabriel looked out the window from his library. "What are the particles in the water? They look like...garbage pellets."

"They're organic." Mom shook her head.

Dad nodded. "It was easy to do once we knew the Lodgers were prone to eating the plastic pellets in the Patch.

We set up a system of tubes that collects petroleum seepage over the nursery and hardens it slightly into pellets with a binding element. Starch, basically. It pumps the particles out in this valley. So they don't need to go up to the Patch."

"It still bothers me," Misty said. "Those pellets kill so many things—fish, gulls, everything. And these creatures *thrive* on them."

Gabriel's mom shrugged. "There's a good chance that they mutated the way they did *because* of the pollution. Anyway, that's the kind of thing we're going to be able to find out."

His dad pointed north. "Nemolab is that way. And we're just a few miles from the nursery, close enough that they'll probably find their way here on their own, plus we'll be helping them. There's a lot to find out."

"Look at this." Mom brought out a tablet and tapped it with one hand as she put on her glasses.

Gabriel took the tablet and showed it to Misty and Peter. It held diagrams of large, composite-polymer tubes and shells of different sizes and configurations. "They're shells."

"Yeah. We figure we can leave them around, nudge the Lodgers toward different shells. This way they're less likely to go off looking for derelict planes and sunken battleships."

Gabriel flipped to the next design. "Needs some color."

They were all gray except for a golden *N* usually around the front "shoulder" of each. He looked out the window into the Lodgers' new valley, where the creatures were feeding, waiting to be understood. "It's too bad, really. I was kind of hoping they'd find the *Nautilus.*"

Misty laughed. "Speaking of submarines, has Nerissa checked in? I thought she'd be here."

"We thought so, too," Gabriel's mom said. She sounded a little—not sad. Defeated, Gabriel thought. "But she hasn't reported in."

Gabriel's dad put his arm around his wife. "If anything had happened, we'd have heard. It would be major news."

"Yeah." Gabriel's mom didn't sound convinced. Gabriel knew Nerissa would turn up sooner or later, though, if only for an uncomfortable dinner.

"We have to get back to the surface by Monday morning," Gabriel said. "It's time for everyone to get..."

Peter rolled his hands in the air. "*To get...* You just sort of trailed off."

"Misty quit." Gabriel looked at Misty and then Peter. "That's not a secret, right? She quit—she, uh, she doesn't like the ... way we handle the truth."

Misty held up a finger. "That's the only reason. I want to go on our adventures. I do." She looked at all of them. "But I can't keep it a secret. Not from my parents. And I can't keep missing weeks of school."

Gabriel shrugged. Misty had done so much more than

she'd planned, and so had Peter. If this was their last adventure as a crew, it was pretty amazing. "So, yeah. We gotta go back, and I guess we lose a crew member. But that's okay, right?" He threw Misty a hopeful glance. "I mean, it's not like we won't *see* you."

"Man, you lay it on thick," Misty said. "We're still going to school together."

"Oh, come on," Peter said to Misty. "*Three days* of school and you'll change your mind."

Gabriel looked at his parents. He wouldn't have them with him on the surface the way he'd had them for the past few days. He'd be alone again with nothing but an empty, sad little house. And then the endless hours in class, waiting for an excuse to get out on the water.

Because they had to be in school.

No, no, no, he finally told himself. There had to be something else; *surely* there was.

"Wait." Gabriel picked up one of his schoolbooks, which he had stuffed onto a shelf in his study next to an old copy of *Around the World in Eighty Days*. He looked at Misty. "*You* want to be able to tell the truth, and you want to avoid missing school. Right?"

"If by tell the truth you mean about nearly getting eaten, then yes."

"I'm not sure if that'll keep happening, but okay, got it," Gabriel said. He looked at his parents. "And you want me in school, to learn about the world of the land and be a, an ambassador." He paused for a moment. "But you know what I want?"

Mom tilted her head toward him, her eyes full of love. "What is it?"

"I want to not be alone." Gabriel looked down at the book and back at his parents. He had to say it once. "I know that sounds...I don't know. Weak. But I love you guys. And I want to see you. I do want to stay close to my friends. And do all the things you want me to do. But seeing you has made me realize that I can't stand another night in that house. So I was just thinking..." He looked at his parents. "Well, what if we were a little less secret?"

Misty asked, "Meaning what?"

Gabriel shrugged. "What if we *were* a school?"

EPILOGUE
A MONTH LATER

The surface of the ocean beaded with shimmering sunlight at dusk, sending brilliant flashes out over darkening water.

Gabriel sat between Peter and Misty as the shiny blue drone boat skipped across the waves. Sheets of ocean spray misted over them as he looked over his shoulder at Mr. and Ms. Jensen and Ms. Kosydar, who sat in the second row. Ms. Kosydar put her hand out and grabbed onto a metal rail that ran along the back of the front seat as the boat flopped.

Misty looked back and put her hand on Ms. Kosydar's.

"It's not far now!" Gabriel shouted. He didn't want the parents to get worried that they'd have to be bouncing along for an hour.

Suddenly he felt unsure that it had been wise to have them all come in a driverless boat. That couldn't possibly make them feel at ease—and he wanted nothing more than for everyone to feel at ease. They *had* to feel comfortable.

Ms. Kosydar nodded gamely as Misty's parents each gave a thumbs-up, when Mr. Jensen's eyes grew wide. "Look."

Gabriel and Misty turned around, and Gabriel gasped. What they saw was as much a surprise for him as it was for everyone else.

They had called it a platform—which in this case meant sort of a floating, unbuilt building of four extremely wide floors and no walls, all held steady on the waves by enormous engines and flotation pontoons under the water. In the center, a stairwell ran up and down the tower, the only thing with walls in the place.

As the drone boat drew closer, he could see his parents standing on the first floor. Both of them looked smart in white coats and black pants, and his mom had her hair pulled back.

The boat slowed and parked itself, and Gabriel's parents helped everyone out.

"I want you to meet my parents," Gabriel said. They introduced themselves as they all tried to hear over the sound of the waves and the wind.

"It's a heck of a place to have a meeting," Ms. Kosydar said loudly, bursting into a laugh as she looked around. Dad gestured for everyone to follow him to the center of the first floor, far from the edge. The central stairwell walls blocked the wind. Now it was almost quiet enough that they could have been inside somewhere.

"It feels strange for us as well," Mom said. She put her hands in her coat pockets and looked out, tilting her head toward shore. "You know, this is the closest I've been to land since before Gabriel was born."

"Really?" Ms. Jensen asked. "Do you miss it?"

Mom shrugged. "Sometimes."

"We wanted you to see it," Dad said, looking at Peter's and Misty's parents. "Where it will be."

"Where *what* will be?" Misty's mom asked.

Dad answered by looking at all of them as he spoke, his voice carrying the smile on his face. He seemed more excited by this idea than Gabriel remembered ever seeing him. Maybe he was looking forward to having Gabriel around. "Look. I know you all heard about Peter, Misty, and Gabriel's discovery. And because of all that, the creatures that they helped will be safe from human interference in a habitat all their own."

The parents nodded, each one giving a combination nod and shrug. They had all heard, but Gabriel was pretty sure that they hadn't heard everything. Which was just as well.

Dad went on, "I wanted to extend the thanks of the Nemo Foundation. But that's not really why you're here. And obviously we didn't invite you all the way out here to enjoy our hospitality." He gestured at their surroundings of metal and concrete.

Mr. Jensen turned around to look toward shore. "At least you have all this ocean. Look—I'm not following this."

"I know, I'm sorry," Dad said. He seemed to try to think of the next words and then continued. "Here it is. We want to create a school. Marine biology. Underwater exploration. Sea conservation. Water rescue. Multi-atmospheric technology." He unfolded his hand, ticking off each one with his fingers. "It would be private, very selective, and the teachers—"

"Would be us," Mom said. "Well, to start."

"Yasmeen and I will be trading off. Spending time here as well as at Nemolab." Gabriel knew this was coming, but still his heart leapt at the thought that they'd be here. *Right here!* He could explore the world of the land without giving up his parents. He could maybe have *both* friends and family for once.

Of course the Lodgers would still need looking after; that was why the trade-off. The Lodgers had so far been satisfied with the imitation Garbage Patch, and some had even come from the Lodger nursery and put on the first of the Nemotech shells. Gabriel wondered if they understood at all that they were under threat if they ventured too far away.

His mom went on, "But the reason *you're* here is we wanted to ask you if Peter and Misty could be the first students. On scholarship, of course."

Peter had obviously only half been paying attention, and now he visibly started, while Misty bounced on her heels.

"They won't be alone," Gabriel's dad said. "We're reaching out across the world. We think that by the time we're up and running, we'll be well stocked with students."

Ms. Kosydar cleared her throat. "But just studying marine biology? Don't you need ... English?"

"Do we?" Peter mumbled.

Mom laughed. "Absolutely. We'll have a full curriculum."

Misty's dad rubbed the back of his neck. "But what about the ... extracurricular stuff?"

"If you mean the submarine," Mom said, "it's all part of the curriculum. But in the open, at least to all of us."

Gabriel watched Misty's eyes. He hadn't known everything his folks were going to say, but he knew the gist, and this last part was key. He had to have Peter and Misty, *had* to have them. But Misty had made it clear: only if they weren't hiding. And this would be in the open.

But what would they say?

"So," Dad finally said, spreading his arms. "What do you think?"

Ms. Kosydar looked at Peter, who was saying so much

yes with his eyes that he was practically shining. "But what are you actually going to *build*?"

"Here?" Gabriel's mom looked up at the unbuilt tower with the sun shining through the bare metal columns. "Oh, I think you'll be amazed."

ACKNOWLEDGMENTS

A lot went into the creation of *Young Captain Nemo*. I had a very simple goal to start with: I wanted to create the kind of story I would have loved as a young person, full of hints and Easter eggs that made the experience worthwhile. Throughout the book, you'll find references to real things like the Eastern Pacific Garbage Patch, which is a nightmare we really do need to solve, and real organizations like the US Navy, NASA, and NOAA, as well as references to bits of lore from Jules Verne. For instance, the island base that the Nemos use is referred to here and shows up in the book *The Mysterious Island*. There are more hidden treasures, but it's more fun not to tell.

I'd like to thank the incredible talent and support of my agent, Moe Ferrara, who shows incredible patience while whipping manuscripts into shape, and my editor, Holly West at Feiwel and Friends, who gamely shepherded this project through its completion. I'm forever in your debt. A lot of this book is pure, unadulterated fantasy, and some is error. Whatever I got wrong is absolutely my own fault. Finally, I'd like to thank my wife, Julia, for her extreme patience, and my daughters, Katarina and Sophia, for inspiring me to create more stories for them. They make me want to be better at every turn.

See you soon, because Gabriel Nemo will return.